From the Graves of Babes

A Novel

By Kevin E Lake

Edited by Stephan Magcosta

In Memory

Philip J. Ables

The greatest story teller I ever knew.

26 June 2020

*This is a work of fiction. The people, places and events in this story are products of the author's imagination. This work, in part or in its entirety, may NOT be reproduced for sale or for free. The author does *not* grant this permission to anyone.

Original Copyright Kevin E Lake 2011

Prologue

He drove slowly through the gray mist on the familiar street. Though it was bright and sunny, all was blocked from view around him due to the fog. His wipers did a violent samba across the windshield, removing the dew that created multiple, miniature rainbows as the sun's light refracted through their moisture.

Pulling into the drive, he grabbed his briefcase, killing the ignition and opening the door. As the car door slammed the front door of the house opened. As the little girl came onto the porch to greet him the fog lifted, the sun broke through and all was right with the world.

"Daddy!" she yelled, running off the porch and jumping into his open arms, his forgotten briefcase dropping to the ground.

"Samantha!" he said, bending over to grab her, swinging her around in the air, now completely free of anything but brilliant radiance and tranquility.

"Push me on the swing," she said, giving him her puppy dog eyes. He could never resist this. He forgot that he had been at the office for twelve hours. His only thoughts now as he carried the girl to the back yard were on all the things he must have done right to be so blessed.

"Tell me all about your day," he said, pushing her higher and higher. "How was school?"

"School is boring daddy," she said, playing it down, pumping her feet to gain more height.

"Why is school boring, Samantha?" he asked.

"Because you aren't there," she said, her words wrapping him around her little finger even more.

"But I'm here now, honey," he said, his heart burning with love for his daughter. "I'm never going to leave you."

"Promise?" she said, looking back over her shoulder, revealing a crooked smile, half baby teeth, half permanent.

"I promise, honey," he said.

He considered her smile the most beautiful he had ever seen. When he had first found out he was going to be a father just over ten years before he had dreaded all the costly expenses that he knew would come, such as braces. He now looked forward to one day accompanying his angel to the orthodontist.

"I'm going to jump daddy," the little girl said with laughter.

"No Samantha!" he screamed, terror rising from the pit of his soul, flooding his heart. This was all familiar now. He could not let her jump.

"Here I go daddy," she said as she came back to him, ready to thrust forward once again.

He tried to catch her. He almost had her but she slipped through his hands.

"No!" he screamed again, as if it would change things, make them different than they had been before. "Don't leave Samantha!"

"Wee!" the little girl yelled as she jumped from the swing.

He rushed forward but he was too late. The empty swing settled back to a slow rock and the thick, darkening fog returned. His daughter was gone forever.

1

"No!" Patrick Hanna screamed, thrusting himself up in bed, waking from the nightmare. His body was covered in sweat, his hands shaking uncontrollably, a combination of terror and acute alcoholism.

Stumbling out of bed he staggered into the kitchen of his Crystal City apartment. Not surprisingly he had left the light on and the bottle of Jim Beam open. Not even taking the time to sit at the table he grabbed the bottle and tugged it hard. It had lost the burning effects and its fire like flavor long ago, going down now as smoothly as water.

Laying the bottle back on the table he took a seat and rested his throbbing head in his hands. Though he didn't sob, tears rolled down his face, plip plopping on the table like rain drops on the ground.

Grabbing the bottle for another swig he hesitated. He looked at it with fear. He knew this was a prison he had built around himself but he didn't know how to free himself from the cell. Throwing the bottle to his lips and jetting his head back hard, he took another violent swig, emptying the bottle of its remaining contents, the equivalent of four shots.

He sat at the table, unable to go back to sleep for hours. Though the liquor was gone he still had plenty of beer in the fridge. What was once dark ambers in his days of only social drinking had been replaced with Bush, offering him more bang for his buck.

He sat as the sun rose over Washington D.C., brilliant rays massaging the rooftops of the buildings around him. Though he was on the tenth floor he could hear the ever honking horns from the cars below. If he were to get to work on time this morning he would have to leave soon. The MCI building that housed his office was not that far away but once the masses started making their way off of the beltway that surrounded the city, it would take him three times as long to get there. This fact did not move him. He continued sitting, holding his throbbing head, crying.

With another hour gone, he grabbed the cordless phone lying on the counter. He called Stacy, his secretary.

"Where are you? I've been covering for you already," she said, a too familiar occurrence. "Tell me you are on your way."

"I'm not coming back," he said, voice trembling.

"Pat. What are you talking about?" she asked, hoping she could talk him out of it once again. This had become a weekly event months ago.

"I mean it this time Stacy," he said. "I can't do it anymore. I'm going home."

"You are home," she said argumentatively. "You need to get in here. Mr. Russell is getting fed up with this. You aren't as valuable around here as you used to be you know."

"Mr. Russell can kiss my…," he trailed off, now searching for the extra strength Motrin that he hoped was still in his cabinet. Finding it he felt relieved.

"Seriously, Pat," Stacy said. "What is going on?"

"You know what is going on," he said, before washing down four white pills. "I can't do it anymore. I have to get out of here. I'm going home."

"Back to West Virginia?" she asked, incredulously.

"Yes," he concurred. "Back to West *by God* Virginia."

"I'll see you when you get here," she said, down playing their conversation up to this point. "You'll change your mind again."

"I'm not changing my mind again, Stacy. I am leaving this time. I'll be gone by the end of the day. Thanks for everything."

She began to offer a rebuttal but it was too late. He hung up the phone and placed it back on the counter.

Walking to the refrigerator he nearly tripped over the empty beer cans lying on the floor. Kicking them out of his way, he opened the door. Looking inside he saw only a pack of smoked turkey, some havarti cheese and a half empty case of beer.

Grabbing a can of Bush, he made his way to the sink, looking out the window at the city below as he opened the can. His mouth watered when it made that crisp, cracking sound. It watered even more as he drew the can to his lips and began to smell its contents, the scent drifting up his nose like smoke up a chimney.

He stopped. His urge to drink was as strong as a bird's urge to fly. Somehow he found the power to begin pouring the precious contents of the can into the sink. He watched longingly as it went down the drain.

"This is alcohol abuse," he laughed to himself, making fun of his actions, not his drinking problem. "If I keep drinking today I'll never get out of here.

The can completely empty, he made his way back to the refrigerator and pulled out the rest of the beer. One by one he dumped their contents down the drain. When he was finished, he had a breakfast of smoked turkey and havarti cheese. This was the first time he had eaten solid food before noon in months. Though it made him queasy to do so, he continued eating until the food was gone. He didn't see the need to leave it to rot.

When he had finished eating he began packing. He would not change his mind this time. He could not stay in this area. Too many bad things had happened. He had to get away, back to the only place on earth he had ever known peace.

#

With all of his sparse belongings packed by mid morning, he loaded them into his four door, four wheel drive Dodge Ram 2500 and began his exodus from the city. He had known this truck was impractical for his surroundings and needs when he had bought it new a year ago, but he thought that at the time he was subconsciously planning his escape from the rat race. As Lily Tomlin has been credited for saying, "Even if you win it, you're still a rat." Exiting the city now, taking advantage of the late morning lull in traffic, he knew that this had indeed been his plan.

He was quickly out of the city, its skyscrapers disappearing behind him. He was on route 29 south, heading back to his homeland. West 'by God' Virginia as he had gotten so accustomed to calling it. He was amazed at how many people in northern Virginia always got the state confused with "western Virginia." It was as if they had forgotten that the states split during the civil war.

A few hours later he found himself crossing the state line on Interstate 64 heading west, the sun following him on his journey in the afternoon sky.

"Welcome to Wild and Wonderful West Virginia," he said, reading the sign as he crossed the state line.

"County roads, take me home."

2

"Finally made it in to see your dear ol' mother did you?" Patrick's mother Ginny said, coming off the porch to greet her nearly middle aged son with a hug. "Haven't seen you in almost two years. I'm glad you didn't forget how to get here."

"Why don't you try to make me feel bad about it, Mom?" Patrick said, pulling away from his mother with a grin.

"So how long you in for this time?" she asked, looking toward his truck for an indication based upon his luggage, her eyes stopping when she realized just how much he had brought. It wasn't much, as he had given most of his belongings to his x wife Shannon after their divorce a year ago. But it was certainly more than would be necessary for a weekend stay.

"I might stick around for a while this time," he said, looking down. "Don't worry though. I'm going to make myself comfortable up at the cabin."

"That place has rats!" she said, now facing her son once again. "Have you even been up there since your father died?"

"No, I haven't," he said, grimacing at the memory of his father's death. He had died from a massive heart attack only six months after retiring from the local lumber mill. The man had been a workaholic and everyone had always joked of how it would probably kill him to stop working. Everyone, it turned out, had been right. Two years had now passed since his death.

"It would be good for me to get back up in the mountains," he said, justifying his plans. "I have a lot of really good memories of me and Dad up there."

"Well, you are welcome to stay here as long as you like while you fix that old shack up," she assured him.

"I might take you up on that Mom, but I'd like to see what kind of shape it is in first," he said, trying to politely decline her offer. He had come here to get away from remembering the bad parts of his past, the types of things no one should ever experience. He knew that with his mother, these things would eventually be brought up. In the mountains, with no one around, he wouldn't have to deal with it.

"I put a chicken in the oven a little while ago," Ginny said. "It is a little early for dinner but we can eat now if you're hungry."

"That would be great," he said, a smile returning to his face. "I didn't stop for lunch. I just wanted to get away."

Walking in the front door Patrick was instantly bombarded with pictures on his mother's living room wall; pictures he loved, yet pictures that broke his heart. There were pictures of his daughter Samantha everywhere he looked; pictures of her with him, with his parents, with his younger sister Elizabeth, five years his junior. There were even pictures of her with his ex wife Shannon.

"I still miss that little angel like crazy," his mother said, catching him staring. "She was the definition of perfection."

"Yes she was," he agreed, tearing his eyes away from the framed memories. "Yes she was."

"Why don't you come have something to drink while I take the chicken out of the oven," his mother said, knowing he must be hurting a million times more than her in regard to Samantha. "I have Coke and Dr. Pepper."

"Okay," he said, following her into the kitchen.

Opening the refrigerator door he found himself instantly looking for a beer. He knew he would not find one here. His mother didn't drink. His father never had either. He certainly could not blame his addiction on genetics. He blamed it on memories of what had happened, used it as an excuse to make the pain go away, but knew that it didn't work to block the nightmares. He knew that in reality it was adding to his troubles.

Patrick and his mother dove into dinner. Having gone nearly ten hours without a drink he found that he was actually hungry. The comfort of being in the home he had grown up in added to his ability to eat as well. He decided that he had definitely made the right choice in coming home.

"So did something happen at work?" his mother asked, half way through dinner.

"No," he said, pausing in mid chew. "I just couldn't stand to be up there anymore. I couldn't stand the rat race and all I do is think about Samantha," not realizing he had now opened the door to Pandora's box.

"Have you heard anything else in regard to the investigation?" Ginny asked, seeing this as an opportunity to ask the questions she knew her son hated to hear.

"I haven't heard anything new in a year," he said, disgruntled. "It seems like they did as much as they could do for the first six months, then they just gave up. I guess with all the children that go missing in this country every day, they have their hands full."

"Do you ever hear from Shannon?" she asked, knowing she was treading on treacherous ground.

"Never!" he said sternly. "I don't want to hear from her either. She should have never taken Samantha to the park that day. If she was going to, she should have kept her eyes on her!"

"You can't blame her forever you know," his mother said. "She is hurting just as badly as you are. She probably blames herself every day."

"She should!" Patrick said, putting a bare chicken leg down on his plate. "I blame her every day!"

"That is never going to get you anywhere, son," Ginny said. "You will never heal."

"Heal?" he said, eyes wide. "How does anybody heal from something like this?" He got up, wiped his hands on a paper towel, placed it beside his plate and started toward the door.

"I'm sorry, Patrick," his mother said, getting up behind him.

"Don't worry about it, Mom," he said, stopping in the living room, realizing he was behaving badly in front of the only person left who cared about him. "I just want to run to the grocery store and get a few things then head up the mountain before it gets too dark," he said, trying to alleviate the tension.

"Okay," his mother said. "But if it's too nasty up there, and you want to spend the night down here and start cleaning that place up in the morning, you can always come back."

"I know, Mom," he said, wrapping his arms around her for a hug. "I really do appreciate everything you have ever done for me. I am sorry that I get so upset when Samantha comes up."

"You don't have to apologize," she consoled. "I think you may have forgotten, but I have two babies of my own. I don't know what I would have done if anything would have ever happened to you or your sister when you were little. I don't know what I'd do now. I worried every day that you were in Iraq."

"I know you did mom," he said. "That's why I sent so many emails. No matter how tired I was at the end of the day I wanted to let you know I was alright." With that he walked out the door.

#

Patrick pulled into the small shopping center in the middle of town. His new truck made the old beaters that surrounded it look even more worn and dated by comparison. He recognized some of the old trucks as their owners had had them when he was a kid. This small Appalachian town, Richwood, West Virginia, was not a place where things changed much, even people's vehicles.

He made his way into the small grocery store. When he was a child in the 1970's and 1980's this store was as busy as could be. However, as technology replaced man power in the coal mines and the lumber industry took a hit at the hands of more fabricated types of home building materials, the town's population began dwindling and now there were no more than half a dozen other shoppers in the store.

"Is that you, Patrick?" the cashier said as he walked by.

"Yes," he said, hesitating, trying to jar his memory. "I'm sorry, it has been so long," he stammered, feeling uncomfortable because he could not remember the woman. She appeared to be roughly his age.

"It's me! Jennifer Ashby!"

"Oh yes," he said. "I remember. We had home room together right?"

"No," she said. "History class. You'd remember me as Jennifer Gates. I'm married now."

"Oh yeah," he said, embarrassed for not remembering. "I'm sorry for my faulty memory. It has just been so long." He truly did remember now but it was more than his memory and the amount of time that had passed that caused him to forget at first. The years had not been too kind to this old friend of his.

She used to be one of the prettiest girls in school, but nearly twenty years and at least fifty pounds had changed that.

"Oh, it's ok," she said, knowing she'd not aged as well as he had. "How long are you in for?"

"I don't know yet," he said honestly, scratching his head with a nervous hand. "I needed to get out of D.C. for a while so I came to spend some time in the cabin up on the mountain."

"Oh," she said. "Well stop in and see me when you're in town. I'll be around."

"I'll do that, Jennifer," he said, starting to head off toward the bread aisle. "I'll definitely be needing to eat while I'm here."

Patrick quickly found the bare necessities to get him through a couple of days; bread, smoked turkey, Velveta cheese substitute (it made him long for the helvarti he could so easily acquire back in D.C.), canned spaghetti, Dente Moore's meals, fruit and bottled water. He found himself afterward passing through the beer aisle on his way to the check out.

"Not here," he said to himself in a hushed tone as he stared at the colorful boxes which seemed to be calling his name. "Leave it behind with everything else." With this, he found the strength to begin pushing his cart once again. He was not going to buy even a six pack.

As he rounded the corner toward the check out he overheard Jennifer talking to another customer.

"Yeah," she said, with a heavy Appalachian accent. "That is Patrick Hannah. He said he's gonna be in for a while."

"That is such a shame, what happened to his daughter a while back," the other lady whom Patrick didn't recognize said in a whisper. Obviously not a very quiet whisper.

"I heard he was in Iraq fightin' terrorists when it happened," Jennifer added.

"Actually," Patrick spoke up, "I was in Iraq overseeing the construction of cell phone towers."

Both women looked at him, surprised by his presence.

"Oh," Jennifer gasped, eyes wide. "Are you ready to check out Pat?"

"No," he thought for a moment. "I forgot something."

He returned to the beer aisle.

"Seems like I can't even leave it all behind here," he said, reaching into the cooler to pull out a case of Bush. He grabbed a cheap, Styrofoam cooler from the top of the beer chest then made his way to the ice bin and grabbed two bags.

"May as well keep 'em cold," he said.

"Will this be it Pat?" Jennifer asked, embarrassed, as she rang up his last item.

"I guess so," he said, not making eye contact, apparently flustered.

"I'm sorry you heard that," Jennifer said sincerely, handing him his receipt.

"I'm used to it," he said, crumpling the receipt, throwing it into one of his bags before heading out of the store.

#

Patrick wasted no time driving back to the edge of town and heading straight up the county road that led to the top of Fork

Mountain. The mountain was called this because it was in the middle of the two major Forks of the Cherry River, which came together in the middle of his childhood town.

As he ascended the mountain, the small town below grew out of site and out of Patrick's mind. He was looking forward to the solitude he would find at his final destination. Solitude like he had never found anywhere in the world.

Arriving at the end of the county road, he placed his truck in four wheel drive then started the last leg of the drive to his cabin. It was only a mile up this beaten trail, not much wider than an ATV trail, but the going would be slow due to the terrain and the condition of the road. No matter how hard he and his father had always tried to maintain the road, every spring led to erosion that would severely damage it. It was not uncommon to have snow fall of four feet at a time on top of the mountain. When it melted, the runoff made the trail seem more like a river than a road.

Patrick was happy to find that though he hadn't been here in a couple of years, there were no fallen trees in the way and he could completely navigate the trail in his truck. If he had come up in a two wheel drive vehicle, it would have been a different story. With the forest's canopy as thick as it was, the road never got enough sun to completely dry. His truck made new ruts where old ones had been. His tires were sinking at least eight inches into the ground.

Pulling up to the cabin he finally felt the sense of relief he had hoped to find. There were no people around for miles now, except maybe one.

The cabin itself sat at the edge of a small clearing, half the size of a football field. It had been hand constructed decades ago by a couple of brothers who had lived in it for many years. Patrick's father was able to purchase it in the late 1970's when one of the brothers had to sell it, along with the 30 acres of mostly forested land it sat on in order to pay the legal fees of the other brother. Patrick remembered the men were named Pete and Phillip Ables.

"Those boys sure are strange," the town's people would always say on the rare occasion that the men would actually make it off the mountain. Phillip had a family if Patrick's memory served him correctly, but Pete did not.

Phillip Ables had been convicted of kidnapping and was sentenced to twenty years in prison. Upon his release, Pete died quite suddenly. For a moment, but only a moment, Patrick thought of the irony of how the actions of such a man had driven him to seclusion. Now such a man would be his closest neighbor.

Patrick was sure the ex-convict still lived in a smaller cabin his brother Pete had erected after his brother's incarceration on the remaining acreage the brothers maintained. Whether he was still alive, Patrick did not know. If he were, that would mean that there was at least one more person in close proximity to him. He didn't mind, knowing the old man was something of a hermit who avoided human contact. If he were still alive he would have to be nearly eighty years old by now.

After parking his truck and killing the ignition, Patrick wasted no time in cracking open a beer. He turned it to his lips and it was gone in ten seconds. He sat and stared at the cabin and the surrounding forest, feeling the coolness of the beer in his throat and stomach. Before opening the door to get out, he grabbed another beer and drank it almost as quickly as he had the first.

Grabbing a third beer, Patrick finally got out of the truck . Instead of grabbing a load of luggage or his groceries, he walked to the middle of the small field in front of the cabin. He held so many memories here. He looked around and, save for the over grown grass and weeds, it looked the same as it always had.

There were fifteen apple trees in the field, branches broken from where black bears climbed the trees every July to get apples not yet ripe enough to drop to the ground. The bears knew that if they waited for them to drop in August, which it now was, they would be forced to share them with the numerous deer that lived in the area. The only apples left on the trees were the ones too high for the bears to reach. This had been the scene here for as long as Patrick could remember.

There were three Maple trees in the middle of all the apple trees. Peter and his father had run a power line from the old cabin to one of the trees where they had fixed a light about ten feet up the trunk. Here they would sit outside for evening meals, using the light when the sun went down.

After cherishing his memories for a moment, Patrick made his way to the front door, removed the padlock, then used the key to the door and let himself in. He wanted to have an idea of the condition of the cabin.

Walking in he was immediately hit in the face with the smell of must and mildew. He could tell that his work would be cut out for him as far as cleaning the place up and making it habitable went.

Grabbing a lighter from a drawer in the kitchen, which was the first room in the cabin upon entering from this end, he lit an old oil lamp that sat on the kitchen table, the words "Standard Oil" engraved on its base. Taking up the old relic, he used it as a light to investigate the rest of the cabin.

Walking from the kitchen, Patrick entered the living room, the only other room in the down stairs section of this two story cabin. It had a wood stove in it that did its job so well, that even in sub zero temperatures in the middle of a West Virginia winter, one had to be careful not to put too much wood in the fire or he would have to go outside to cool off. There was also a couch, a recliner and a coffee table in this room. Oil lamps sat on small end tables at each end of the couch. Patrick lit these for more light.

Though there were two windows in this room, it was now dusk outside and light in the cabin was scarce. The electricity could never be counted on as reliable due to the ferocity of the West Virginia winters and the fact that the cabin was so remote. When the lines would get snapped from falling limbs, it always took the power company until the following spring to fix them.

Seeing that the cabin was pretty clean so far, the only nescience seeming to be the odor, which should be easily remedied by opening all the doors and windows to allow the cabin to air out, he decided to head upstairs. He walked over to the makeshift wooden ladder that was nailed to the wall on the opposite side of the wood stove, a couple feet behind the couch, and started his ascent.

Popping his head into the first of two upstairs bedrooms he looked around cautiously before committing himself fully. He wanted to make sure there were no critters such as raccoons or squirrels waiting to pounce on him as he entered. He saw none so he continued his climb.

Likewise, the upstairs was still in pretty good shape considering the amount of time since anyone had been in the cabin. He found that in the bedroom above the kitchen, the roof had been leaking for some time. There was mildew and mold around the ceiling and a stain on the floor. Luckily the water had come in on the side of the room opposite the bed. Patrick could only imagine the reek and mess that would be involved if the water had been absorbed by the goose down mattress that was on the bed, similar to the one on the bed in the other room. Both beds were full size, and though very old, they were very comfortable.

Realizing he had finished his beer, Patrick decided it was time to go back to his truck and bring in his belongings, thereby enabling him to grab another drink. He carefully made his way back down the ladder and out the door he had come in through the kitchen. There was also a back door to the cabin that exited the far end of the living room and went into the back yard, which was about the size of a basketball court, before giving way again to deciduous forest. Other than a half acre field about one hundred yards through the woods, up the hill from the cabin, the rest of the thirty acres that made up the property was wooded.

Before grabbing any luggage to take in, Patrick grabbed beer number four for the evening, cracked it open and started to drink. He then took all his groceries in and laid them on the kitchen table, returning to his truck for part of his luggage only after making sure to put the rest of his beer on ice in the inexpensive cooler he had bought at the store.

As Patrick grabbed what he had decided would be the last of his luggage that he would carry in tonight, he hesitated as he noticed one of Samantha's dolls in the back seat of his truck. It had been her favorite, a cabbage patch kid that he had bought her when she was only five years old. It was a gift to her after yet another of his long business trips away from home during his twelve year stint with MCI.

Grabbing the doll, he took it inside. He put his luggage in a neat pile in one corner of the living room, the doll gingerly placed on top. Though it was not too cool, he decided to light a fire in the wood stove, just for the sake of reminiscence, to remember all those times he had come up here with his father.

#

The fire burning nicely, Patrick unrolled his sleeping bag on the couch. His intentions were to drink himself to sleep like he had done almost every night over the past year and a half. He had had such a hard time when his father had died a couple of years back, but when Samantha had gone missing just a couple months after that, it was more than he could bear. The demise of his marriage would soon follow. He would sell his house and move into that entrapping apartment in Crystal City, and he would stay drunk, more than likely losing his job next if he had not chosen to quit today.

A dozen beers into his case of twenty four, Patrick laid on the couch and shut his eyes. He hoped that for just one night he would not dream of his daughter. He hoped that the new location he was in would change his horrible life, give him a cure by relocation. The log in the stove simmered to a dim glow and Patrick slept.

Outside it was dark. The moon was full and owls hooted while other night birds and what had to be millions of tree frogs made their strange sounds. A slouching, dark figure made its way through the woods to the edge of the small yard surrounding Patrick's cabin. He had come from the direction of the small field on top of the hill above the cabin. He set up a collapsible, nylon folding chair just inside the wood line, facing toward the cabin. He cracked open a thermos of coffee, poured himself a cup, and waited.

"Knock Knock Knock," came the light pounding on the front door of the cabin.

Patrick's eyes opened. He could see the sun shining through the two small windows. He felt relieved knowing he had made it through the night without a single nightmare. He had no idea though who would be at the cabin door on top of this secluded mountain.

"Hello," Patrick said, opening the door, seeing no one when he did.

"Hello," a small voice came from the little girl on his porch step. "Would you like to buy some girl scout cookies?"

"What?" Patrick said, looking down to meet the little girl's eyes. She seemed to be about ten years old. She was wearing a girl scout uniform.

"How did you get all the way up here?" he asked, amazed.

"My name is Sarah," she said, ignoring his question.

"Well, it is nice to meet you Sarah," Patrick said, not believing a girl this young would be brave enough to walk all the way through the woods by herself, or that any parent would let her. Not to mention that the mountain was so steep that even an adult in good physical condition would get a heck of a workout by doing so. "I would love to buy some girl scout cookies. How much?"

"Fifty cents," she said, holding out a box of thin mints.

"Is that all?" he said, eyes widening, sounding amazed. "I thought they were like, three dollars or something?"

"That is too much money for a box of cookies," Sarah said.

"Ok," Patrick said, walking out the door, making his way around the little girl. "Let me get a couple of quarters out of my truck."

"Do you live here now?" Sarah asked, following him.

"Yes," he said, opening the driver side door to his Dodge and grabbing two quarters from the console.

"Do you have any kids?" she asked, oblivious to his situation.

"No," he said, looking down as he handed her the quarters in exchange for the box of cookies.

"Are you sure?" she asked, staring him straight in the eyes.

"Why would you doubt me?" he asked curiously.

"I can sense things," the little girl said, still staring him in the eyes even though he was having a hard time maintaining eye contact with her. "You seem like someone who would have kids."

"Well I don't," he said dismissively. "I have a lot to do around here today. I need to fix this place up so I'd better get started. Will you be ok to walk back from here? Can I give you a ride?"

"I'll be fine," she said, starting to walk off into the woods, not heading toward the road.

"Shouldn't you take the road?" Patrick asked, concerned.

"I know a shortcut," Sarah said, starting to head through the woods in the direction of the half acre field above his cabin. Patrick couldn't imagine how a short cut could be in that direction since it headed toward the very top of the mountain, not down toward the main road.

Patrick watched until she was out of site, hidden by brush. He then went back in the cabin, walked through the small living room and into the kitchen to place the girl scout cookies on the table. As he did, he noticed something out of place. Samantha's cabbage patch doll was sitting on the kitchen table.

"I thought I left you in the living room . How did you get in here?" he said, picking up the doll, carrying it back into the living room and placing it on the end of the couch.

"Yes, I have lots to do today," he said to himself, plopping back on the couch. "But it can wait. I need more sleep, this is supposed to be a break anyway."

With that Patrick laid back down, his head by Samantha's doll, and was quickly back to sleep.

#

Patrick wasn't sure how much time had passed when he awakened but he knew he felt much more rested than he had when his sleep had been interrupted by the girl scout selling cookies.

"Weird," he said, scratching his head, still finding it odd that a little girl would be selling girl scout cookies all the way on top of Fork Mountain. How had she even known anyone would be here? He surmised that word still spread quickly as it always had in the small town below.

Deciding to get right to work on the leak in the roof, Patrick headed outside to the old tool shed that lay at the edge of the yard. He and his father had always kept enough tools and materials in it to fix anything that might go wrong with the humble dwelling. He quickly unlocked the combination lock, though it panged at his heart to do so. When he had set the combination years ago, he used the numbers 1129. This stood for November 29'th, Samantha's birthday.

"Note to self," he said, placing the opened lock on the door hinge. "Get a new lock."

Talking to himself was something that had become commonplace for Patrick in the past year. He knew that if anyone ever caught him doing so, as his secretary Stacy had several times, they might think he was crazy. He cared not though because he knew that after going through what he had in the past couple of years he actually had lost part of his mind. Who wouldn't?

Taking the aluminum extension ladder out of the shed, he carried it over to the side of the cabin that bore the leak, extended it to the proper length, leaned it against the cabin, then climbed to the top of the roof to survey the area. He wished to assess the damage before needlessly carrying supplies up the ladder that might not be required.

Making it to the top of the roof, he immediately found the damaged portion. There was a bit of a tree limb that had punched through. He looked back down and noticed that the majority of the limb was lying shattered on the ground below. Peering up, he saw where the limb had broken off of a large white oak. Had the limb fallen a few feet further over, the damage would have been much worse.

It didn't take much effort to pull what remained of the limb out of the roof. He tossed it to the ground with its original portion and decided he would cut it into firewood later.

Climbing down, he went to the shed and gathered a few boards, some left over roofing from when he and his father had roofed the cabin shortly after they had acquired it twenty years before, and piled the materials at the foot of the ladder. He then returned and did the same with the shovel, hammer and nails that he gathered from the shed.

He decided first to get something in his stomach. He was not under any time constraints now. Moving slower was part of his goal in coming back to West Virginia.

Glancing at his watch he saw that it was only ten o'clock. He determined to have a bite to eat, fix the roof, then go check in with his mother so she would know that he made it through the night. He also wanted to politely decline her offer of letting him stay with her as the cabin was certainly suitable for him. He would be able to get more done up here anyway, not having to go back and forth, up and down the mountain; particularly more drinking.

Walking back into the cabin and into the kitchen, he decided that he would feast on girl scout cookies. It wasn't healthy, but it couldn't be any more harmful to him than his liquid diet that had become so common over the course of the past year and a half.

Making it to the kitchen table he could not believe his eyes. Samantha's doll was once again sitting on top of the table.

"What the…?" he said, picking up the doll. "I know I haven't left you here once and now I've found you here twice."

Glancing back down at the table he noticed too that there were no girl scout cookies.

"Who's here!" he demanded, turning quickly to head into the living room. "Are you up there?" he said, peering up the hole to the upstairs.

He wasted no time in quickly climbing the wooden ladder to the second floor.

"I know you're in here," he said, trying to sound brave, as his trail foot left the top step of the ladder and planted firmly on the floor. "If you wanted the cookies back all you had to do was ask," he said, believing Sarah was still around somewhere.

Using the light coming through the windows he could see that no one was in this room. He cautiously made his way into the second bedroom. This room was empty as well. Looking up, he could see a small ray of light coming through the ceiling from where he had removed the limb.

"She must have taken the cookies and ran," he said, determined he was alone.

He made his way back down the steps and back into the kitchen. He opened his foam cooler, where he had laid his lunch meat and cheese substitute on top of his beer the night before. He took it out to make a sandwich. Though he could feel the Bush in the cooler calling to him he resisted the temptation. He was determined not to drink until after he had checked in with his mother.

He quickly made a sandwich and gobbled it down. He decided to have another and ate it only slightly slower. He realized he could get used to having solids for breakfast again. Maybe this change would be good for him in more ways than he realized. Maybe now he could let go of his addiction, as he hoped to let go of his pain and anguish.

Making it back outside he wasted no time in carrying his materials to the roof, doing so in two trips. People at his office at MCI would never believe he could be quite the handyman on an old cabin high atop the Appalachian Mountains. He had been in sales and management for the communications company ever since starting there upon his graduation from West Virginia University back in 1996. However, the fact remained, he was a hillbilly long before he was a businessman. As the saying goes, 'you can take the boy out of the mountains but you can't take the mountains out of the boy.'

#

"That should do it," he said, pounding the last nail one last time.

After climbing back down from the roof Patrick put the ladder and his tools back in the shed. Ordinarily, being in the area and only going to be gone for a short while, he would not lock the shed. However, since he had already been visited by what he believed to be a curious little girl with sticky fingers, if not someone else, he decided to lock it.

He then went into the cabin to make sure the back door was locked from the inside before heading out the front door and locking it from the outside. Before leaving, he had decided to take Samantha's doll and lay it squarely in the center of the couch, facing outward.

"There," he said, making a mental note. "I know exactly where I've left you now and you'd better be there when I get back."

#

"Back so soon?" his mother Ginny said as he walked through her front door.

"I just wanted to check in," Patrick said, intentionally avoiding the pictures of his daughter that decorated the walls. "The place isn't in too bad of shape so I won't have a problem staying up there."

"Well you're right in time for lunch," she said, motioning him toward the kitchen.

"I just ate actually," he said, trying to decline. His mother was always trying to feed him. She always had. If it hadn't been for the fact that he had spent half his childhood gallivanting through the woods and along the river banks he was sure he would have been fat in his youth.

"You can have a cup of coffee then while I eat my lunch," she said, refusing to let him simply check in with her then leave.

"Okay," he said, eyes rolling, agreeing to join her.

"So the place is habitable is it?" Ginny said, just before taking a bite of her left over chicken sandwich.

"It is in better shape than I thought it would be," he said, sipping stale coffee. "I was prepared for the worst, was hoping for the best, and got something in between."

"That's nice," his mother said, taking another bite.

"I had a visitor this morning," he informed her.

"Up there?" Ginny asked, surprised. "I've been up there a few times myself but it has been so long ago I don't know if I would be able to find it now. Who came to see you?"

"Of all things," he began, "A little girl selling girl scout cookies." He took another drink of coffee. "Her name was Sarah."

"Really?" his mother said, voice trailing, eyes going toward her sandwich.

"Do you know who she is?" he asked.

"No," Ginny said, pondering. "I don't suppose so."

"What do you mean you don't suppose so?" he asked, feeling as if she was holding something back.

"There hasn't been a girl scout troop around here since your sister was a little girl," Ginny said, appearing to be thinking about taking another bite but unwilling to commit. After another moment's hesitation she continued eating.

"I remember that," Patrick said, smiling, reminiscing. "You were the den mother. Once a week I would hide in my room while all those little girls were here."

"You had a hard time of it too," Ginny giggled. "Half of them had a crush on you and the other half were just good at hiding it. You were in high school and they just thought you were the coolest thing since Velcro."

"I was," he said, both of them laughing.

"Does Elizabeth still come by all the time?" he asked, changing the subject.

"Oh yes," she said, rolling her eyes. "I'm only fifty nine now but she is convinced that she is old. She still comes by every weekend to make sure I haven't fallen and can't get up."

"It would be nice seeing her again," Patrick said after taking his last swig of coffee. "Do you expect her this weekend?"

"She's already committed," Ginny said after gulping down her last bite. "I called her last night and told her you were here. She is coming over as soon as she gets off work on Friday."

"She's still the guidance counselor over at Nichols County High School?"

"Yes, she is," Ginny concurred. "She loves that job and her students seem to love her. They voted her 'coolest teacher' the past three years in a row, even though she isn't a teacher."

"Great," Patrick said. "She was always such a neat kid."

"I could have her bring one of her old girl scout friends," Ginny said with a teasing grin. "They are all in their late twenties now you know."

"That's the last thing I need right now, Mom," Patrick said, playing off the jest. "I want to focus on getting to know myself a little better and determine where to go from here, not spend my time getting to know someone else, as lovely as they may be."

"I'd better be off," Patrick said after a few minutes of small talk. "I am going to swing by the library and take advantage of their free wireless internet service and check emails."

"I have dial up, here," Ginny said, pointing toward her archaic desk top sitting on an old desk in a corner of the kitchen.

"Uh," Patrick began, choosing his words so as not to be offensive. "I know you have dial up. I can get done in half the time on my laptop with the wireless at the library and head back up the mountain. I imagine there are some folks who want to know where I am and why I'm here so I'll have to put out some fires. Maybe on down the road I'll use your dial up."

"Maybe down the road," Ginny began, walking with him to the door, "You'll realize your back in West Virginia and out of D.C. and you'll learn to relax. The only big deals are the ones you make. It's hard to make them around here."

"That's why I've come back," he said, hugging her with a smile before leaving.

#

Three minutes later, as the town was small enough to travel its entire length in only five, Patrick was at the Richwood Public Library, which sat beside the city hall. He went in, found a secluded table in the back by the reference section and pulled his HP laptop out of its case. He wanted to touch base with the few friends he had left at MCI to explain why he had taken his sudden hiatus.

Not surprisingly, his inbox was full; questions from friends. He wrote and recopied to all a simple response: 'I had to get away. I am not coming back, but I will stay in touch. I am in Richwood, West Virginia… more later. All is well.'

"Patrick Hanna!" he heard the lady say with a touch of shock in her voice.

"Heather?" he said, looking up, recognizing her instantly. How could he forget? She had been his highschool sweetheart. He had stared into those big brown eyes many times, and they hadn't changed through the years, though they now bore new lines along their edges.

"What on earth are you doing here?" she asked, taking a seat across from him.

"Checking emails. What are you doing here?" he asked, never breaking eye contact, not hiding his excitement.

"I work here," she said, getting comfortable. "I don't mean what you are doing at the library. I mean what are you doing in Richwood? The last I heard of you, you were some big shot in D.C."

"I was hardly a big shot," he said, chuckling. "I was working there for MCI. I had to get out of the rat race so I came back to the best place I could think of to do so. How long have you been working here?"

He had gotten used to changing the subject over the past year and a half when people would ask about his personal life. He always tried to head them off before they could ask about his daughter.

"I've been here for a few years now," she said, looking down slightly. "Me and Ken got divorced a while back and I had to start working."

"Sorry to hear that," he said, sounding sincere. However, the human side in him felt a bit less than sincere since Ken was the guy Heather had started seeing when he had gone off to college. She and Ken were both a year behind him in High School. Distance may make the heart grow fonder, but back then, Heather had found Ken's proximity attractive.

"Well," she said nervously, readjusting her posture. "It is what it is."

"Yeah," he agreed. "I guess so."

"So how long are you in for?" Heather asked, now changing the subject herself.

"I believe for quite a while," he said, taking a serious tone.

"Are you staying with your mom?"

"No," he sighed. "I am staying up at the cabin."

Heather knew the cabin well. When they had dated in high school, the two of them went up there almost every weekend. Never so much to camp, as to make out in a place they knew was very secluded, where they never had to fear intruding headlights pulling up behind them as they did what young lovers do in the back seats of cars on the weekends, or in their case, in the cab of Patrick's father's truck.

"That place always kinda gave me the creeps after that one night," Heather said, recalling a memory that Patrick was all too aware of. He had never forgotten and had thought about it from time to time.

In the fall of his senior year, Patrick and Heather had gone up to the cabin as they had so many times before. However, this was a particularly clear, crisp night and there was a meteor shower in progress.

Instead of parking beside the cabin as they always had, they decided to drive up the short, steep hill above the cabin. They parked, turned off the motor and held each other, peering up through the windshield awaiting a heavenly show of streaking lights.

However, in a matter of minutes they both felt very uneasy, as if someone or something was watching them. Several times Patrick kicked on the headlights, feeling as if someone were standing right in front of the truck.

The first time, he didn't say anything when he did this and Heather was silent as well. The second time he did it, only minutes later, Heather mentioned that she felt something too.

After flicking the lights on a third time and seeing nothing, the couple decided to get out of the field and head off of the mountain all together. Though they would head back up the mountain to be together in private many times after that, they were always sure to get out of there before dark.

The strangest thing about that night would happen one bright, fall afternoon a couple years later. After they had spent half a day on the mountain deer hunting, Patrick's father was ecstatic about showing Patrick something he had found in the woods, on top of a small knoll about twenty yards into the woods from the field.

"Look at these," his father had said.

"Look at what?" Patrick had asked.

"These sunken holes with triangular rocks at the ends," his father had continued. "These are sunken graves. They must be over two hundred years old."

Patrick surveyed the area, and sure enough, there were no less than eight sunken spots in the ground. Each of them had triangular rocks at both the heads and the feet. The holes were facing east to west. His father had without a doubt discovered an abandoned, unmarked grave site on top of Fork Mountain.

Over the years Patrick and his father would ask many of the old timers in town about the graves yet no one seemed to know anything about their origins or who might be buried in them. Patrick had all but lost contact with Heather by this time, due to Ken, and he had never told her of this discovery.

"Yeah," Patrick said, recalling the memory, deciding not to enlighten her of the graves now either. "I spent last night up there but I hadn't thought of that. I'm glad I didn't or I probably wouldn't have stayed. Thanks for reminding me," he finished with a chuckle.

"I didn't mean to scare you," Heather said. "I have thought about it through the years myself. It is one of the strongest memories I have of those days."

"I was sorry to hear about your little girl," she said, after both of them had gone silent, thinking back on that night. "I hate to bring it up, but I wanted to let you know that I was thinking about you."

"Thanks," he said, looking down, voice trailing. "Yeah, it is a hard topic to avoid, especially with people I haven't seen since it happened. I try not to think about it though." He thought about it all the time and doubted anyone believed him when he said he didn't.

"So do you have a boyfriend?" Patrick asked, definitely in want of a different topic. "I don't mean to sound forward. I was just curious as to how you are doing."

"I was dating a guy from Summersville," she said, mentioning the town at the other end of the county, twenty five miles away. "Turned out he was dating a girl in Beckley at the same time." Beckley was another forty miles on the other side of Summersville.

"Some people," Patrick said in dismay.

"I guess I used to be one of those people, huh?"

"Oh, I didn't mean it like that," Patrick shot back quickly. "I had forgotten all about that," he lied.

"Well," she began, looking apologetic, "I was wrong back then, and I was very stupid. Looks like I got what I deserved."

"Heather," he began, his best Dr. Phil impression. "We were just kids back then. We didn't know what we wanted and we thought thirty was old. Don't beat yourself up over something that happened half a lifetime ago."

"I wish I could be more like you," Heather said. "I still hold grudges against Ken. He left me for another woman and never comes and sees our son Caleb. He sends money, but he says he just doesn't want to deal with it."

"Not a kid person I take it?" Patrick asked, one eyebrow raised.

"Caleb is blind," Heather said. "He had lots of problems as a baby and the doctors doubted he'd live to see his first birthday. He has lived to see ten of them, but he lost his sight in the first year of his life."

"Is he otherwise healthy?" Patrick asked, concerned.

"Yes, thank God," Heather sighed. "I love that kid so much. We've been through so much together."

"Well it sounds like you know all about tough times too," Patrick said, realizing he was not the only one in the world with problems. "You and Caleb should come visit me at the cabin sometime," he said, not thinking before speaking. He had come here as a way to avoid people, and now he was inviting his girlfriend from so long ago and her child he'd never met to come visit him at his place of solitude.

"As long as we leave before it gets dark," Heather laughed. "I don't know what was going on that night nearly twenty years ago, but I don't want to repeat it."

"How about Saturday then," Patrick said, again surprised at how committed he seemed to have his mountain top solitude broken.

"Okay," Heather said. "Let me talk to Caleb about it and make sure we don't have anything else going on."

"Like there is anything going on around here," he mused.

"I know, I know," she said, rolling her eyes. "Just come back in later in the week and I'll confirm. I'm sure it won't be a problem."

Heather already knew her day was open. She was just making Patrick come in later in the week so she could see him again. Her feelings for him never went away completely though eighteen years had passed, literally half her lifetime. She hoped he felt the same to some degree.

"Alright then," Patrick said as he began packing up his lap top. "I'll come back later this week, perhaps more than once, and we'll see if we can get together without any paranormal interruptions." He said this smiling, yet still feeling a bit queasy in the gut at the memory of that night.

"It was really good seeing you again," Heather said, having walked Patrick to the door.

"The pleasure was all mine," he said, walking backward out the double glass doors. He made it to his truck, got in, and looked up as he started the engine to find Heather still staring at him through the library's glass doors. When their eyes met, she waved and he did the same just before pulling out to head back up the mountain.

#

Patrick pulled up to the cabin and wasted no time going inside. The entire drive up the mountain he had been thinking of that night nearly twenty years ago when he and Heather had had their experience. Of what they were never really sure. For some reason, thinking of this had made him think about Samantha's Cabbage Patch doll and her mysterious "movements" around the cabin.

Making his way quickly to the living room, he felt at ease to find the doll sitting exactly where he had left it.

"It had to be the beer," he said. "Speaking of which…"

Patrick made his way to his cooler in the kitchen and grabbed a can of Bush. This was officially the first day he had waited until mid afternoon to have a drink in many months. Cracking the can open, he guzzled its contents, taking it all in only three deep, strong swigs. He had gotten to the point in the past six months especially of his drinking, to where he could just keep his throat open, able now to drink an entire can in only three gulps.

"That was so good I think I'll have another," he said.

Grabbing another can, he opened it and took his time with this one. He loved the feeling alcohol brought to him. It seemed to be the only thing to take off the "edge." It took about four beers to get this feeling of calm yet it quickly left, replaced thereafter by intoxication.

Still thinking of the night in the field, Patrick decided he would walk up the hill through the woods and visit it. He stuffed a beer in each of his two back pockets and headed out the door, not locking it behind him.

He walked casually, at an easy pace as he made the one hundred yards trek to the field. The trail was wide enough to get a truck through yet he and his father had usually walked to it in the past.

Patrick loved the smell of the fresh air on top of the mountain. The area was nowhere near as humid as his home in northern Virginia had been, though the grade of the climb still caused him to sweat.

Coming to the field, Patrick stopped just as he entered it, surveying his surroundings.

There was an old building that had all but fallen to the ground now sitting off just to his right. This building had been used by the Ables brothers years ago for their gardening equipment. Patrick and his father had never actually gardened on the mountain and therefore never maintained the old building. Looking at the eye sore that it now was he was wishing that they had. He journeyed over to the fallen remains.

Looking in through where a wall used to stand, Patrick could make out some old glass bottles scattered on the ground. Picking one up, a clear glass, one gallon jug, he noticed the word "Duraglas" on the bottom, the word made out of risen glass itself.

"You might be worth something," he said. "I'll have to look you up on eBay."

Looking around through the rubble he noticed two more just like it. He also noticed half a dozen bamboo cane rods that had at one point been hanging on the wall of the fallen shed. He never knew why they would be up here, bamboo coming mostly from Asia. Who would have bamboo on top of a mountain in West Virginia and what on earth would they use it for? Fishing poles back in the old days perhaps?

The field itself, grown up with waist high weeds from mid-summer through fall, was once again in such rough condition. Bees and butterflies made their way gaily from flower to flower. Though the weeds themselves were an eye soar, their flowers and the critters that loved them looked quite beautiful.

"I think I'll have a garden next year," he said, crushing his now empty beer can with one hand and tossing it into the mess heap that was the old building. "I'll come back for you later," he said, pulling another beer out of his back pocket before starting to walk across the field. He walked in a stretched out, stomping fashion, using one foot at a time to take down the largest of the weeds in front of him.

"I love Halloween," he said after taking a sip from the freshly opened Bush. "If nothing else I'll plant a bunch of pumpkins, just for fun."

Memories of the past were now rushing through his head. These were not the same depressing memories however, involving Samantha and her disappearance. He was now remembering all the times he and his father had come up here and spent quality time together, something that was rare in his childhood, his father having worked so much.

This field is where Patrick had perfected his shot with a rifle. Every summer since he was ten, he and his father would bring their Remington .243's up here to sight in their scopes for the upcoming deer season. They would also bring their .22 magnums and do the same in preparation for the fall Turkey season.

Most people used shotguns for turkey hunting, taking advantage of the pellet spread to better hit their target. However, the mountains were so steep, so up and down in this part of the Appalachians that you could literally see a flock of turkeys that may only be one hundred and fifty yards away as a crow, or a bullet flies, but often being on the next knoll over, they were actually three hundred yards or more away as far as walking distance. These birds, being able to see in color, detect movement like a sniper, and having peripheral vision that extends to forty five degrees behind their heads, Patrick and his father preferred the rifling ability of .22 magnums. They knew they could never sneak up on the birds to get a shot off with the much less distance capability of a shotgun.

Though he felt that he had never been as close to his father as he could have been, Patrick had loved him and certainly missed him now. He had told himself growing up that he would never allow his own work later in life to interfere as much with his own relationships with his children should he ever have any. However, genetics and learned behaviors are hard to escape and sure enough, when he had become a father himself he missed out on too many opportunities with his daughter because of work.

Now he began thinking of Samantha and feeling guilty. He was thinking especially of when he had agreed to go to Iraq as an independent contractor for MCI to oversee the construction of cell phone towers during the occupation.

"It's only for a year," he had told his wife Shannon. "And they are going to pay me twice as much as they would if I stay here. The first $85,000 of it is tax free too since I am making it on foreign soil."

Shannon had hated the idea from the start. She and Patrick had met in her home town of Hattiesburg, Mississippi shortly after he had started working there after college. He had come on as a junior sales rep.

Shannon was interning at MCI, being a business major at the nearby College of Mississippi. The two had met in Patrick's first month on the job and their love affair instantly began, heating up quickly. Patrick had never wanted to get married until he was well established and in his thirties, but this "southern bell" as he used to call her, especially when he mocked her accent, had changed his plans. He proposed to her in only six months.

Shannon herself was so smitten with Patrick that she never finished college. She didn't mind much at the time, knowing Patrick was making enough money for them to be comfortable, but she would later resent him for this fact and throw it in his face often during times of argument.

"It's not about the money," she had pleaded. "You have me and Samantha, and you just moved us to Virginia. We don't know anyone and now you want to run off to Iraq? What if you get blown up by one of those roadside bombs?"

Patrick never thought of the threat of the ongoing war in Iraq or what he might miss out on in regard to his family for a year. The folks at MCI had sold him, the salesman, into believing that upon his return he would certainly be considered for management as he would be in a managerial position in Iraq. He would oversee most of the work, doing very little of it himself.

They had dangled the carrot of $180,000 in front of his face. At his age, he viewed it as the opportunity of a lifetime. Little did he know just how much his life would be destroyed while he was gone.

Deep in thought, Patrick detected movement at the edge of the field to his right. He looked over to see an old man, certainly in his late seventies if not older, limping toward him. This was Phillip Ables.

#

"He came into the library today," Heather said to her friend Jennifer as she was checking out of the grocery store. Girlish giddiness filled her tone.

"That was quick," Jennifer said. "Did he know you worked there?"

"He didn't seem to," Heather said, digging her wallet out of her purse. "He asked me to come up to his cabin this weekend."

"You guys used to spend a lot of time up there back in the day," Jennifer laughed. "I wonder if you'll be doing the same thing this weekend you always did back then?"

"Of course not," Heather admonished. "I'll have Caleb with me," she finished, smiling, as if to elude that would be the only reason why their activities would not be the same as those of the past.

"Remember that creepy story you told me about that place?" Jennifer asked, helping the high school aged bag boy pack Heather's groceries.

"Yes," Heather said, hesitating before swiping her Visa check card. "We actually talked about that today."

"And you're still going?" Jennifer asked, pressing the verification button on the register after Heather had swiped her card.

"I won't be staying after dark," Heather informed her. "I'm sure it was nothing anyway. We were just two paranoid kids, knowing we were up to no good."

"Let me know how it goes," Jennifer said, handing her the receipt.

"Why, so you can tell everyone in town?" Heather said, half joking, half serious. She loved her lifelong friend but she also knew that she had become one of the town's gossips over the years.

"Anything you tell me stays with me," Jennifer said. Heather wasn't so sure how true the statement was.

"I'll let you know what you need to know," Heather said, smiling teasingly.

#

Heather went to Cherry River Elementary to pick Caleb up from school after leaving the grocery store. She loved how the teachers and staff at the school had been able to see that Caleb was integrated into the regular population of the school. Richwood was a small mountain town, with relatively no specialty services for a child like Caleb, but it was a town of caring people who bent over backwards to help their neighbors. All the staff and students at the school had welcomed Caleb with open arms and made him feel like any of the other students.

"How did he do today?" Heather asked Caleb's teacher, Mrs. McClung. Linda McClung had been teaching at Cherry River Elementary School for thirty years. This would be her last year before retiring. She was loved by all of her students, past and present. Many of them from years ago still kept in touch with her to this day.

"He is as good of a kid as his mother was when I had her," Linda smiled.

"Thank you so much," Heather said.

Heather looked toward the back of the room where her son sat alone. However, he seemed to be looking off to the side, his lips moving as if he were mumbling.

"What's he doing?" Heather asked curiously.

"I don't know?" Linda said. "He's been doing that the past couple of days. I was going to mention it to you. I don't know if something is going on that has him worried, but he seems to have been talking to himself lately. I can't make out anything he says. He doesn't do it when I am close. You know, he can't see but he can always tell when someone draws near. Every time I do he stops talking and acts as if he hadn't been doing so in the first place."

"I'll talk to him about it on the way home," Heather said, a look of concern on her face.

"How you doing little man?" Heather asked as she drew close to Caleb. As Linda had said, he stopped mumbling as his mother drew near.

"Mommy!" he exclaimed, standing up and reaching open arms in her direction.

"Are you ready to go home?" she asked.

"Yeah," he said, squeezing her hard.

"See you tomorrow Caleb," Linda said as the two walked past her.

"Bye Mrs. McClung!"

4

"Aint seen you up here in a long time," Phillip Ables said, drawing close to Patrick.

"I've been away for a while," Patrick said, remembering the man from his youth.

"I know the feeling," Phillip said. "I was away for awhile myself. Missed this mountain like crazy when I was gone."

Patrick was surprised that Mr. Ables brought up his own absence. He was quite certain that the old man knew that everyone knew where he had been and why.

"Yeah," Patrick began. "I have thought of this place so much while I've been gone. I couldn't wait to get back. I am long overdue. I am glad to see that not much has changed."

"Yeah, not much changes up here," Phillip said, looking around, as if looking for someone else. "You can tell when even the slightest change takes place; which trees get blown over in wind storms, which banks erode with the spring's thaw."

"I have these woods memorized like the back of my hand," Patrick said. "I'm sure you do even more so. You have been up here a lot longer than I have."

"Yeah," the old man said, scratching his head, a distant look in his eyes. "I've been up here fifty two of my seventy six years. I did four years in the Navy during Korea."

"I never knew you were in the military," Patrick said, trying to ignore the other twenty year period the man spoke of. Patrick, as well as everyone else in Richwood knew he had spent that time in prison.

"Most men of my generation were," Phillip said. "Your service and all is too soon to be forgotten though by folks back here when accusations start flying."

"I was in Iraq myself for a year," Patrick said without thinking. He knew it was not the same, comparing his time spent in a war zone as a highly paid civilian contractor to time spent as a seaman.

"Which branch?" Phillip asked, his attention returning to the present.

"I was a civilian contractor with KBR," Patrick said, feeling less important in comparison. "I worked for MCI actually but we got our contract through KBR."

"Oh yeah," Phillip said, his voice trailing off. "I've read about those guys. They make ten times the money providing the services to the military that we used to provide for ourselves."

"Yes," Patrick said. "I was actually overseeing the set up of cell phone towers," he finished, trying to separate himself from the guys who do the cooking and cleaning the soldiers used to do for themselves, while at the same time fighting the war. "I guess the world has changed a bit since your days in the military."

"I guess a lot has changed," the old man agreed. "Ya know, 'ol Ike warned us this was comin' on his way out of office back in my time. This 'military industrial establishment' he called it. That is why I like this mountain so much. Nothing up here ever changes, just the seasons."

"So I take it you live in the small cabin over in the next hollow?" Patrick asked, changing the subject.

"Yeah," Phillip said, looking in the direction of his small home. "I come over here quite a bit though. I guess even though we sold the place to you and your dad all those years ago it still feels like home to me."

"I would imagine," Patrick said. "I don't have a problem with you being over here. Last time I checked, you were the one always kind enough to let us come up here and hunt before we even bought the place."

"Sorry to hear of the passing of your father a while back," Phillip said.

"Thanks," Patrick said, looking down at his now empty beer can.

"I heard about your daughter too," Phillip said.

"How did you hear about that?" Patrick asked, looking up quickly.

"Even I get off of this mountain top every now and then," Phillip chuckled. "I've been here my whole life, except those twenty four years, and people in this small town know everything about everyone who's ever lived here. Almost everyone," voice trailing off again.

Patrick had no idea what this last statement meant.

"I can relate to your pain though," Phillip began again. "I had one child, a daughter. She died while I was in prison."

So the one ton elephant was out from under the rug. Phillip had mentioned prison. He cared not to hide the facts. Facts that he was sure Patrick knew already.

"Was she sick?" Patrick asked, having not known of the death of Phillip's daughter. He could remember that he had had a daughter, several years older than him. That is all he could remember.

"She was afflicted by a close relative's illness I guess you could say," Phillip said, now peering back toward the hollow in which his little home sat. "She was actually nineteen when she died. She got to grow up at least, but that's still awful young to check out."

Not knowing exactly what the old man was talking about in regard to a disease, Patrick did not fish for any more information. He knew talking about his own experience was difficult enough and he was sure it was equally painful for the old man. He thought it was ironic though how they had both lost the love of their lives while they were gone and could do nothing to stop it.

"If you ever want to stop in to chat, feel free," Patrick said, bringing the conversation to an end. He was now out of beer and wanted to get back to his cabin and grab another.

"I'll do that," Phillip said. "Likewise, if you ever need anything you know where to find me."

The old man then began to walk out of the field, back in the direction from which he had mysteriously appeared.

"Oh," he said, turning around to face Patrick, as if he had forgotten an important piece.

"Yes," Patrick said, turning back to face the man, as he himself had also started to leave.

"If you see anything strange up here, anything at all, let me know," the old man said in an eerie tone.

"Like what?" Patrick asked.

"Well," the old man began, looking down as if in deep thought. "You'll know if it happens." He turned once more and began to leave.

"Weird," Patrick said to himself, heading back to the cabin. "I need another beer."

#

Phillip Ables made his way back to his small rickety cabin on the other side of the hill. He went inside and sat in the small, one room dwelling and stared at a picture on the mantel.

The picture was that of his ex wife and his young daughter. They both had long brown hair and the most beautiful big brown eyes he'd ever seen.

His wife had divorced him his first year in prison. She said she could not stand being married to a man who had done the evil things he had been convicted of doing. Try to convince her as he did, she would never believe that he was innocent.

She had stayed on the mountain with Phillip's brother Pete. While in prison, thoughts of how the two might be spending their lives together, sharing his daughter as if she were THEIR daughter kept him up so many nights those first fifteen years. Other thoughts of his daughter kept him awake at night to this day.

He had been in prison with only five years remaining on his sentence when he got the news. It seemed his daughter, nearly twenty at the time, had drowned in a local swimming hole. He was not even allowed out of prison to attend her funeral. His ex-wife left the Richwood area shortly after, going to stay with extended family members she had in Virginia.

As he stared at the picture, a mouse scurried out of the wall above the old rock fireplace onto the mantle, sniffing the frame. Phillip grabbed his .45 caliber pistol. He opened the chamber and loaded a special bullet, one he had re-loaded himself. It had ten small beads in it and not much powder. He used this type of bullets for such occasions as this.

He raised the pistol, following the mouse with the gun's sites as it hustled away from the picture. He didn't want to destroy the only picture he had left of his daughter.

He followed the mouse down the fireplace until it made its way to the floor.

BANG!

The shot rang out and the mouse was dead. There were now a few more small indentations in the floor, left from the shot, to go along with the many others.

He let the mouse lay dead, now staring once more at the picture. Life was not fair. He had been dealt a bad hand. Nothing it seemed had worked out for him, yet he had not given up on exacting his revenge.

#

"Who were you talking to in class today Caleb?" Heather asked her son as they pulled out of the parking lot of Cherry River Elementary.

"Just one of my friends," he said, staring out the window, though he could not see the passing scenery.

"What is your friend's name?" she asked, a questioning look on her face her son could not see.

"Sarah," he said.

"Who is Sarah? Is she a new girl?"

"No," he answered, turning toward her. "She doesn't go to my school. She just stops by to see me sometimes."

"Do the other kids talk to her?" Heather asked, concerned.

"No," he said. "They can't see her."

"Why not," she asked, getting more curious by the second.

"They can't see what I see."

"What do you mean honey? That doesn't make much sense."

"Why not?" Caleb asked. "I can't see what you can see. You don't question that."

"I guess you're right," Heather said, admitting he had a point.

"Do you see Sarah anywhere else?" she asked as she turned left into hospital bottom, the neighborhood in which they lived that derived its name sake from the fact that the local hospital was located here. It had now been closed for more than a year. The town was dying so much that there was not enough business for even the hospital to stay open. If anyone needed medical attention they had to go to Summersville on the other side of the county.

"No," he said half heartedly. "She just started showing up at school a few days ago."

"Where does she live?" Heather had not yet determined if Sarah was simply an imaginary friend or something she should be more concerned about. For the time being she decided to tread lightly until she knew for sure.

"She said she lives on the mountain," he said.

Heather knew not which mountain to which he was referring. He could be speaking of Fenwick Mountain, heading west out of town. He also could have been referring to Hinkle Mountain, which overlooked the town, named after the Hinkle family who had been in the area for more than one hundred years.

"She said I'll be seeing her again soon," Caleb added, facing away from his mother. "She said I'll get to see where she lives."

"Ok kiddo, we're here," Heather said, pulling the car into the driveway. "I'll help you in."

Heather helped Caleb to the door as always, though it really was not necessary. She had done well raising a blind child. She never rearranged anything in the yard or in the house. Caleb could maneuver around their property and in their home almost as if he could see. Consistency was very important in their lives.

As Caleb made his way to his bedroom Heather went into the kitchen to prepare dinner. She decided to whip together some spaghetti for simplicity. Her life was so chaotic as a single parent of a blind child. She had learned to keep things as simple as possible years ago.

She thought to herself about how if things went well, they might not be so simple in the near future. She was still smitten about having run into Patrick at the library. She really had to fight the urge to call him and let him know she would love to join him for the weekend. She didn't have his cell number, but was sure she could get it from his mother who she had remained acquainted with like most people in her small town. She wasn't sure if his cell would work on top of the mountain.

Could Caleb have been talking about Fork Mountain in regard to Sarah's home? Of course not. No one lived up there except Patrick. Patrick and that weird old man who had served time for doing terrible things to children. She made a mental note to herself to keep an extra eye on Caleb when they went up there now that Phillip Ables back on the loose.

#

Only five miles distant, yet seemingly a world away, Patrick sat alone at his small table in the dimly lit kitchen of his small cabin. He ate sandwiches for dinner, washed down with cheap beer, making a mental note to himself that he would definitely have to buy a wider variety of food tomorrow at the grocery store. Perhaps some liquor at the drugstore.

As he sat eating, he stared at Samantha's doll sitting on the couch in the other room She was still exactly where he had left her.

Thoughts raced through his half drunken mind. These were thoughts of his new life, secluded on the mountain. He was tickled that he had run into Heather today. He had to admit that it was true that your first love never dies. He had actually thought about her off and on through the years.

When he and Shannon had had problems, even before Samantha's disappearance, he often wondered what life would have been like if things had worked out with him and Heather. Even during the good times he found himself thinking about how things might have been different. Maybe he would find out now.

He thought too of his run in with Phillip Ables. The man had always seemed harmless to him in his youth and he was quite taken back all those years ago when he had heard the news of what had supposedly happened. There were plenty of times when Patrick was a child that he himself was alone with the man. He had never felt threatened. Nothing had ever happened.

His brother though; that was a different story. The man had never threatened Patrick or acted inappropriately. He just gave him the creeps. Maybe it was the way he looked at him and never said much of anything. Nothing to fear now though, as the man was dead. He didn't know the specifics of the circumstances surrounding his death, only that he was dead.

Whatever Patrick's feelings of uneasiness around Pete Ables, they were not a worry now. Dead men can do no harm. Could they? Of course not. Patrick was finding that one of his nemesis from D.C. had followed him here; time. He now had too much time to think here as well.

His thoughts were turning back to Samantha now as he stared at her doll on the couch. Samantha never got to see this cabin or this mountain top. Patrick was sure she would have loved the place. She was such an excitable, curious child. There were not too many experiences that she didn't enjoy.

"I need another beer," he said as he got up and walked toward his cooler. "I need another beer."

As evening shifted to night the shadows of the forest on top of Fork Mountain lengthened, blending together to form a blanket of darkness. Yet again, as he hoped he wouldn't do, Patrick drank himself to sleep. Without the sounds of the busy D.C. streets below he would find that bed time would come much earlier for him while living in such seclusion.

At the foot of the mountain Ginny flipped aimlessly through channels on her flat screen television. For years, the Fox News Channel seemed to be all that was ever displayed on the screen as her husband watched all the headlines of the day and the conservative talk programs. Though a blue dog democrat his entire life, he most often voted Republican, yet refused to switch parties, like so many in West Virginia, in fear that their ancestors would haunt them from the graves each election season for having done so.

It wasn't that she couldn't find anything to watch. Her mind was filled with racing thoughts of the conversation she had had earlier in the day with her son. She worried about him, like all mothers do, regardless of how old their children get. But there was a part of the conversation that had her deeply concerned. The part when he mentioned Sarah, the girl scout.

There was good reason Ginny had been the girl scout's den mother when her daughter Elizabeth was involved with the group. Fear!

Before Patrick was even born, let alone Elizabeth, there had been the story of the local girl scout that had gone missing. Ginny could not remember her name, but she remembered the story well. It happened in the early 1970's and it was the talk of the town through the entire decade. By the mid 80's, when Elizabeth was a scout and Ginny the den mother, the talk had subsided but the memory remained among members of the older generation.

Ginny knew that Patrick drank too much. He hid it well, but a mother always knows. Through the years she had received numerous late night phone calls from him while he was still in D.C. after Samantha's disappearance. The calls become more frequent after Shannon had left and gone back to Alabama. Many of the calls Patrick never remembered. She eventually quit answering the phone if it rang after mid-night.

Though she never drank herself, save for the rare occasion of New Year's or her son's wedding, she had been around people who drank in excess. She had an older brother who she had painfully watched ruin his life with alcohol. She even felt guilt at times, fearing Patrick may have picked up the addictive gene from her side of the family.

She was fully aware of the fact that when people drank in excess regularly, their minds often played tricks on them. She knew too that during times of detoxification, when people tried to get sober, paranoia and fear often set in, as well as delusions. She witnessed her brother go through such bouts of paranoia, fear and delusions during several failed attempts at sobriety.

Still, she thought it was quite ironic that Patrick would mention the girl scout. No one knew exactly what had happened to her because they never found her body. Then there were the others. The town eventually calmed down a bit with the incarceration of Phillip Ables.

The story was that Phillip's brother, Pete, had grown suspicious of his brother and gone to the authorities. The man was convicted on hearsay more than any hard evidence. No evidence at all was even presented at trial.

There had been a couple of witnesses, parents of some of the missing children, who had noticed the Ables brother's truck casing out their neighborhood not long before their children disappeared. The town was so small though, that at any given time anyone could be accused of having been casing out a neighborhood. You had to pass through virtually all of them to get anywhere. The parent's were obviously under duress and wanted a scapegoat.

Phillip's conviction came in the days long before DNA testing. The word from his own brother and a handful of distraught parents cost the man twenty years. Not a long time for a child killer but a long time it seemed for a man who had no evidence presented against him.

The thoughts of Pat and his problems and his run in with a girl scout that so resembled a missing girl from nearly forty years ago weighed heavily on Ginny's mind. Try to shake them as she did, she could not. She found herself turning the television off and looking for old photo albums in the hall closet.

She sat and flipped through pages of old Polaroids from the mid 1970's. Most of them were of her and Patrick. It would be several more years before Elizabeth would show up. She eventually made her way to these pictures as well, seeing the advancement of technology as Polaroids gave way to brighter, clearer pictures of cleaner paper generated from disposable cameras.

Even further into the albums the pictures gave way to those of Samantha, printed from her computer's printer. How much easier it would have been for her to have gotten more pictures of her own children had she had the use of digital cameras when they were young.

She found herself wishing that there was more she could do to help her son in his time of pain. She knew alcohol was not the answer he needed, though he kept trying to find the answer with its use. She knew that with each empty can of beer, or every empty bottle of liquor he was only making his problems worse.

Perhaps there was something she could do? Perhaps there was something Elizabeth could do? She was a counselor at the high school on the other side of the county. Perhaps there was something Elizabeth would know to say that could help.

With this in mind she picked up the phone and called her daughter. She was really reaching out for any straw she could grasp. Hopefully she could find one that worked.

#

The next morning Patrick found himself getting up earlier than usual, more than likely due to the fact that he had gone to sleep earlier than usual the night before. He decided to get more work done on the cabin today, but only after having a real meal. Turkey and cheese sandwiches had gotten old. He chose to drive off of the mountain and have breakfast at his mother's house.

He threw a black trash bag, only half filled, mostly with empty beer cans, in the bed of his truck then got in and started the engine. He stomped on the brakes only a second after starting to roll backward. He had glanced in the rear view mirror and saw a little girl run into the woods behind his truck. It looked like she might have actually been jumping off of his rear bumper. It also appeared as if she had taken his bag of trash.

"What the?" he mumbled to himself.

He put the truck in park, turned it off and headed into the woods where he thought the child had gone. He walked, stopped and listened, then began walking again. He could hear nothing when he stopped.

"Is anyone out here?" he yelled through cupped hands.

"They aint gonna talk to ya unless they want to," the old man, Mr. Ables said from behind him.

Patrick turned to see Phillip Ables sitting in a folding chair, a coffee thermos resting on the ground beside him. He had been so caught up on seeing the little girl with his trash that he had blown right by him without even noticing him.

"Who isn't going to talk to me unless they want to?" Patrick asked, seemingly oblivious to the oddity of the old man sitting in the woods overlooking his cabin.

"The chillin'" he said.

Patrick knew that Phillip meant "children." Patrick himself used to speak with a typical Appalachian American accent. An education and years spent out of the state did a good job of taking it out of him.

"You saw her too?" Patrick asked.

"I seen her," the old man said. "I see 'em all the time. That there was Trixie. You'll be missin' something' if she's been around."

"Do they live in the hollow there?" Patrick asked, referring to the half dozen homes that make up the small, almost clannish community at the end of the trail which led to his cabin. The community was a good two miles on the mountain above town. Rumor was that the community was settled by some moonshiners during prohibition. Four generations later the folks living there were still quite removed from mainstream society. They were the salt of the earth; kind, generous and friendly. But their eyes were always on anyone who passed through their community, their guns in hand, hidden behind their window frames. "And what do you mean something's missing?"

"Them chillin' don't live nowhere now," the old man said, rising to his feet, taking up his chair and thermos. "I call 'er Trixie cause she's always playin' tricks. Mostly she takes things. No worry, you'll find whatever it was. The others usually make her give it back."

Phillip giggled to himself, obviously thinking of some of the pranks that Trixie had played on him in the past.

"She took my trash!" Patrick said incredulously, wondering why anyone would want to take a bag of beer cans.

"She'll take anything," Phillip chuckled again. "They aint the ones ya gotta worry about though," he said, serious now.

"What are you talking about?" Patrick asked.

"You never noticed none of these things when you were up here as a kid did ya?" Mr. Ables asked.

"What things?" Patrick asked. "I don't understand anything you're talking about."

"You ever experience anything outta place up here before this time?"

Patrick thought for a moment. The memory of him and Heather parking in the field, then leaving so soon out of fear due to the creepy feeling they had came to mind. He didn't mention this to Phillip Ables though.

"No," he decided to lie instead.

"Well ya seein' things now aint ya?"

"What things?" Patrick asked.

"Like Trixie a takin' somethin' out of the back of your truck. I bet if ya think hard enough ya can come up with something else that's gone missin'.

Patrick thought hard for a minute. He thought back on the girl scout cookies that he knew he had bought from Sarah. Could Trixie have taken them?

"Ya had a cute little girl try sellin' ya girl scout cookies yet?" the old man asked with a snicker.

Was Phillip reading his mind?

"Yes," Patrick said. "That's Sarah. I met her my first morning up here. I thought maybe she lived close by but I've found out recently there are no girl scout troops here anymore."

"She used to live nearby," the old man said.

"Where does she live now?" Patrick asked.

"She don't live nowhere," Mr. Ables said, drawing near Patrick, invading his personal space.

"She's homeless?" Patrick asked, voice filled with pity.

"No," the old man whispered, looking around and taking a pause before looking Patrick square in the eyes.

"She's dead!"

"You are off your rocker old man," Patrick said, stepping back to put distance between the two of them.

"You couldn't see 'em when you were a kid," the old man said, ignoring Patrick's insult. "Something's happened to you as a man. Something has broken your spirit. It was the disappearance of your daughter!"

"Why do you say that?" Patrick asked, growing angry.

"Because ya gotta be broke to see 'em. Healthy, happy people can't see and feel these things. When you get broke, you are able to channel things around ya differently. Almost like the things can tell you're broke and they seek ya out. Its like they want to be seen."

Patrick was confused. He didn't know what to think. He knew he was broken. He was not going to attempt to deny that. But was there another way Phillip might have known he was a bit troubled? Patrick had no idea how long the man had been sitting out here or how often he did it. Perhaps he was spying on him? Maybe he'd seen him drinking or heard him talking to himself.

"I've dealt with that," Patrick lied again. "That's in the past. I've moved on."

"Bah!" Mr. Ables spat on the ground. "There aint no movin' on after something' like that."

"I have to get off the hill," Patrick said, beginning to back away from the old man again. "I'm having breakfast at my mom's. Then I have some work I need to do."

"Don't be scared of the chillin'," the old man said. "When you see the other, get the heck out of his way. Better yet, come get me."

"Who is the other?" Patrick asked, flattering the old man. He was still convinced in his mind that there were just some curious little kids making their way too deep into the forest.

"You'll know when he's around," the old man said. "All hell will break loose when he comes around."

With that, the old man started walking away himself. He was off to his little cabin to catch up on sleep. He had indeed been out all night pulling watch above Patrick's cabin. Not spying on Patrick, but looking for "the chillin'" and for the one who makes all hell break loose.

#

"You're out and about early," Ginny said, noticing that the clock in the living room read only seven thirty as she opened the door.

Patrick was still trying to wrap his brain around the conversation he had just had with Phillip Ables. The man had seemed so normal the day before, making no mention of "chillen" or "the one that makes all hell break loose."

"I got to sleep earlier last night," Patrick said, making his way past her. She could smell alcohol on him as he passed. She assumed he had tied one on the night before.

"So what do you have planned for the day?" she asked, following him to the kitchen.

Patrick grabbed a pan from under the cabinet, set it on the stove top, then began pulling eggs out of the refrigerator.

"I'm eating a real breakfast for one thing," he said, placing three eggs on the counter top before spraying the now warm pan with Pam. "Sandwiches just aren't doing it for me anymore."

"What's next?" Ginny asked.

"I'm going back to the library," he said, helping himself to a cup of coffee that would be stale soon. "I am going to do some research."

"Uh huh?" Ginny responded, in a tone expressing her disbelief.

"What does that mean?" he asked innocently, making his way to the stove to flip his eggs before placing two slices of bread in the toaster.

"I guess you found out yesterday that Heather works at the library," she mocked.

"Oh yeah," he said, playing it off. "It was nice running into her again."

"I bet," Ginny said, giggling.

"That was a long time ago mom," he said defensively, lightly lifting his eggs out of the pan and placing them on a plate with a spatula. "We both have completely different lives now."

"Yeah," Ginny said, taking a seat across the table from him, as he was now seated and was vigorously eating his eggs and unbuttered toast. "You both just happen to be single again too."

"I'm not here for that mom," he said, sounding defensive once again.

"I know," she said, "but it would be a nice fringe benefit of being here don't you think?"

"Are you trying to pimp me out mother?" he asked jokingly, trying to lighten the mood.

"Of course not," she said. "But I remember how much you loved that girl when you were young. You didn't even date anyone for a year after the two of you broke up."

"Yeah," he said, finishing his eggs, drifting off as if in deep thought. "That sure was a long time ago though."

"Well, who knows what might happen," she said.

"So what are you doing today?" he asked, trying to change the subject.

"Oh, I'm glad you asked," she said. "I am cooking dinner for Elizabeth tonight. We talked last night and she said she couldn't wait till the weekend to see you so she is coming over today when she gets out of school. I hope you don't have plans."

Patrick did not have plans but he felt a bit panic stricken. This meant that he would have to wait until after dinner to start drinking. Though he truly wanted to quit, or more so "get it under control" as he hopelessly thought he could do but knew he could not, he had not waited until that late in the day to start drinking in more than a year.

"I guess I can come," he said hesitantly.

"You don't sound very excited," Ginny roused. "You haven't seen her in two years."

"Yeah, I know," he said, looking for an excuse. He took a long, slow sip of coffee to buy time, searching for words. He couldn't fool his mother though. She knew him too well. "I was hoping to get some more work done on the cabin today, but I guess all I really have around here is time. Sure, I'd love to make it. What time?"

"I would say around five," she said.

"Ok," Patrick agreed, rising from his chair and placing his plate and now empty coffee cup in the sink.

"I'll wash that," Ginny said, noticing he wasn't even making an attempt.

"Oh, sorry," he said, turning back toward the sink.

"Seriously, I will," Ginny chuckled.

"Alright then," Patrick said. "I guess I'll head off to the library now. They open at eight. That way I can get done early. I have to go by the grocery store and buy some real food. I guess I'll come back off the mountain around four thirty."

Patrick walked into the Richwood Public Library, a swagger in his step in case a certain librarian was watching, and made his way to a table in the back. He wanted to ask for Heather but decided instead to play it cool. He powered up his lap top and began checking emails.

"You're in early," Heather said, coming around the corner, her arms full of books she'd been returning to their shelves.

"I wanted to get a jump start on the day," he said, minimizing his screen. "How ya doing so far today?"

"Ok," she said, laying the pile of books on the table and taking a seat, this time beside him instead of across from him. "Always the same 'ol thing around here. Put books back on the shelves first thing in the morning. Most of them are late. People always return the late books in the drop box at night to avoid the fines for a while longer."

"I'm not surprised," Patrick said, a light chuckle. "So are you up for Saturday?" he asked, not wanting to sound too bold, but seeing no need in wasting time.

"Sure," she said. "Me and Caleb have nothing going on. I think he'd really enjoy the mountain air."

"It's good for everyone. I've been enjoying it myself."

"I bet," she said. "I've been to D.C. once and I don't know how anyone could stand living there."

"Now you understand why I got away," he said. "People used to tell me I was crazy for wanting to come back here, but if they'd spent time up there they'd understand."

"Yeah," Heather agreed. "I guess for most of us who've always lived here, the desire to leave is pretty strong. It seems like so many Richwooders end up coming back when they get older though."

"Yeah," Patrick said. "Again, I don't know how long I'll stick around, but this sure is a great place to recharge the batteries."

Patrick and Heather talked for a while, then she returned to her work. Patrick answered a few more emails, checked the news headlines then made his way to the grocery store.

He bought the usual; lunch meat, bread and beer, then headed back to his truck. This time he was happy that he was not the center of any whispering rumors in the store. At least none that he overheard.

Instead of driving back up the mountain he decided to check out one of his favorite childhood hang outs instead, Rudolph falls. He wanted to be sober when he met with his mother and sister for dinner and he feared that if he were to be alone on top of the mountain with his ice cold case of Bush that he'd be drunk by five o'clock and either miss dinner or make a fool out of himself if he went. So instead of going past the now long closed Exxon station, through the neighborhood of Mill Town and back up Fork Mountain, he went left and headed about a mile out of town to the banks of the North Fork of the Cherry River.

Rudolph Falls was named after the man, Mr. Rudolph, who had donated the land to the city in the mid part of the last century. He had sold the rest of his land to a local timber company.

There was a small concrete dam built across the river above the falls. It was the place where the city obtained its drinking water. Below the damn there was a set of naturally formed sandstone falls. They weren't big by any means, but they made the perfect natural slide into a swimming hole of about eight feet deep below.

The hole itself was formed so that even in the summer months, when the rivers were practically dry due to lack of rain, the hole still held enough water in which to swim. At a depth of six feet at its lowest level, the hole was about thirty feet in circumference.

Patrick maneuvered his Dodge down the little dirt road that led to the bank. He got out and made his way to the water's edge. He stared into the clean mountain water and noticed half a dozen native brook trout milling around in the depths below.

"Nice day for a swim, huh?" he heard the female voice come from the other side of the river. He looked up, surprised that he hadn't noticed the young lady until now. She would have been hard to miss in any situation. She appeared to be barely of age and was stunningly beautiful. Her shoulder length brown hair was wet, matted to her head. Her face, fare and of perfect complexion, revealed the most beautiful pair of big brown eyes. She wore a bikini top and a pair of running shorts. She sat, knees up toward her chin, on a rock. She was leaning up against a moss covered log.

"I hadn't really planned on it," Patrick said. "It would be nice to cool off a bit though."

"The water is perfect," she said. "You should get in."

The invitation was hard to decline. Patrick took off his shirt, kicked off his sandals and emptied the contents of his pocket. His wallet was in his truck but he was carrying his cell phone. He laid it underneath his shirt, alongside his sunglasses that he had taken off the top of his head.

He waded knee deep in the water. It was about ninety degrees and humid for this part of the country yet the water was ice cold. It had been meandering its way through miles of shaded forest, coming out of natural springs halfway up the mountain. Deciding it would be best to dive right in, he did just that.

Though cold as it was, the water was refreshing. He swam to the bottom, eyes open, looking for the fish he had seen from the bank. They were long gone. He swam the entire width of the hole, crossing to the other side, surfacing only feet away from the young lady sitting on the rock.

"You're right," he said, wiping the water off of his face as he stood once again knee deep. "I didn't realize how hot it was."

"My name is Amy. What's yours?" the young lady said.

"Patrick," he said, washing the cool mountain stream's water over the hair on his arms. "You can call me Pat though, everyone else does."

"Are you from around here?" she asked.

"No," he said. "Well, kinda. I grew up here in Richwood. I've been away for about twenty years. Are you from here?"

"I'm just traveling around," Amy said. "I've been here for the summer and I like to come up here and swim."

"Oh," Patrick said, deciding not to pry any more. He had learned over the past couple of years not to offer any information about himself that wasn't asked for. By respecting other people's private information he had found that they generally did the same. That way certain topics, particularly the issue of Samantha, never came up.

"So how long are you going to be around?" Amy asked.

"Maybe for a while this time," Patrick said. "I have a cabin up on top of the mountain and I've come in to fix it up a bit and spend some time alone. I've been in Washington D.C. over the past few years and I wanted to get back to the serenity of the mountains."

"What mountain is your cabin on?" Amy asked, a bit of concern in her voice.

"Fork Mountain," he said. "Do you know it?"

"Yes," she said, looking down and to her right, as if recalling a memory.

"This town sure has changed a lot in the past twenty years," he said, breaking the ice further. "How old are you?"

"Nineteen."

"Oh," he said. "You looked a little older. I would have thought early twenties."

Amy stared at him, emotionless.

"I didn't mean that you look *old*," Patrick back tracked. "I mean, early twenties is still young. You just seem a bit mature for nineteen."

"Don't worry about it," she said.

Patrick climbed out of the water and took a seat beside Amy. They talked of things insignificant for a while, neither revealing much about themselves. As they talked, the bright, sunny sky began to fill with dark, ominous storm clouds.

"We have to get out of here," Amy said, sounding worried.

"Do you need a ride somewhere?" Patrick asked.

"No," she said. "I'll just go up to the hotel and wait out the rain then head into town."

The Four Seasons Lodge and all of its twenty rooms sat above the swimming hole. The hotel did little business throughout the year except during the week of the town's annual homecoming festival in August.

"I don't mind giving you a ride into town, or wherever you're staying," Patrick said.

"No, it's ok," Amy said. "When the rain stops I might come swimming again."

Amy was being evasive. Patrick did not know why.

"Ok," Patrick said, before diving back into the river and swimming across to the other side, again underwater. When he surfaced this time the rain had already started. He slipped on his sandals, grabbed his shirt and headed for his truck. When he opened the door, he looked back to see if Amy was following. She was already gone.

"That's strange," he said, looking up the hill. It was at such a steep angle, he could barely see the roof of the hotel. "She must have hightailed it up there to get out of the rain."

The rain was now starting to come hard so he got in, closed the door and started the engine. He decided he'd wait out the storm at his mother's house. Again, he feared being alone at the top of the mountain with his ice cold case of beer.

"Did ya get wet?" Ginny asked when Pat came through the door.

"Yeah," he said. "But mostly from swimming. I went up to the falls and jumped in for a while."

"You still have plenty of clothes you've left here in your old bedroom . You haven't gained a pound since college. I'm sure they'll still fit."

"Yeah," Patrick said.

He went into his old room and slipped on an old pair of nylon running pants. They read 'Mountaineers' down the leg. You couldn't grow up in West Virginia without being a West Virginia Mountaineers fan. The school usually boasted a pretty good football team but seemed to choke in bowl games. Some people referred to it as the 'Don Nelan curse,' after the name of one of the former coaches. Nelan had been one of the longest and winningest NCAA coaches in history but he never seemed to pull off wins in the big games.

Patrick and Ginny sat around and talked of old times. Around four o'clock Ginny started cooking dinner; deep fried chicken, mashed potatoes and gravy, green beans and corn. The dinner was an Appalachian favorite.

"Hey Pat," Elizabeth said as she came in the door half an hour later. She made her way directly to her older brother, giving him a giant hug.

"Hey, kiddo," he said. "How have you been?"

"Good," she said. "I stay busy with work, but I guess we all do. How have you been?"

"I've been ok," he said.

"So mom tells me you're staying for a while this time?"

"Yeah," he said, making his way back into the kitchen to take a can of coke from the refrigerator. "Want one?" he offered.

"Sure, why not," Elizabeth said.

The two sat in the living room and talked of things inconsequential while their mother set the table. They had learned years ago not to offer to help. Ginny took pride in partaking in what she felt were motherly chores.

After the table was set, the three of them sat around it and started eating.

"So how long do you think you'll stay?" Elizabeth asked.

"I don't know," Patrick said. "When I decided to come I just wanted to get out of D.C. I never really put any thought into the next step. I'm not even going to think about it for a while. I'm just going to enjoy the break."

"Well ya know," Elizabeth began. "If you wanted to get involved with anything, there are a ton of kids in this county that could use a positive male role model. You could volunteer to coach a sport down at the high school or something. I have lots of contacts there. I know the decision makers over at the board office too."

"I might do that later," he said, lifting the deep fried chicken skin off his plate and sticking it in his mouth. "You know I have high cholesterol?"

"I figured you would," Ginny said. "Your dad had it bad and never did anything about it. That's one of the things that led to his heart attack."

"I know," Patrick said. "My doctor told me to take the skin off of my chicken before I eat it. So I do," He said, plopping the skin in his mouth and chewing vigorously with a smile.

"I doubt that is what he meant," Elizabeth said.

"Well, I hope you didn't start smoking in Iraq," Ginny said. "I know all the guys in the Army seem to smoke. You didn't pick that up over there did you."

"Oh no," Patrick said. "A lot of the civilian contractors I worked with did it too. Most of them were former soldiers. That is one habit I always thought was disgusting.

"Drinking is bad for you too," Elizabeth said.

So that is what this was all about, Patrick thought. He chose his next words carefully.

"I drink occasionally," he said. "Who doesn't?"

"As long as you can keep it under control," Ginny said. "You know your uncle Mike started out drinking occasionally and we all know what happened to him."

"Yeah," Patrick said, reaching up to scratch his head uncomfortably. "I know. I keep an eye on it. I just like to relax with a beer from time to time."

"A lot of people tend to drink too much instead of dealing with their issues," Elizabeth said. "All it does is bury the problem."

"I need to get up the hill," Patrick said as he rose to his feet. "I don't want to be getting up there after dark."

"Pat," Elizabeth said, standing as well. "I didn't mean to…"

"I know," he said. "I just need to get up there. There's still some daylight left and I can get a few things done. I haven't even started mowing the field."

"I'd like to come up there and visit some time," Elizabeth said.

"Really?" Patrick sounded surprised. "You never wanted to go up there back in the day."

"I know," she said. "I was a girl. What kinda girl wants to go hang out in the woods? I'm older now and have been taking on more of an appreciation of the beauty of this area. Any time I've been gone due to travels I've missed it."

"Ok," Patrick said. "Anytime you want to come up is fine with me."

"I'll give you a call in a few days," Elizabeth said. "Do you still have my number in case you want to call me?"

"Unless you've changed it," he said. "I have it in my cell phone," he said, reaching into his pocket. "Oh, it must still be in my wet shorts."

He made his way back to his old bedroom. Taking up his damp shorts he saw that his phone was not there.

"Darn it," he said. "I must have left it at the river."

"I'm gonna run back up to the falls before I head up the mountain," he said as he entered the living room. Elizabeth and Ginny had made there way there from the kitchen. "I think I left my cell phone at the river."

"Ok," his mother said, arms open for a hug. "I guess I'll see ya again soon huh?"

"Yeah," he said. "I'll stop in tomorrow if I come off the hill. If I don't then, I'll stop the next time I'm down."

"When you want to talk about anything just give me a call," Elizabeth said, also hugging him.

"I will," he said. With that he was out the door.

Patrick made the quick drive back to Rudolph falls. He was upset to see that his phone was not where he had left it. He decided to walk up the trail leading to the Four Seasons Lodge.

"Hey, did anyone bring a phone up here that they found by the river?" he asked the lady working the front desk, recognizing her as he finished his question. "Nikki? Is that you?"

"Hi Pat!" the beautiful lady in her mid thirties said. Nikki and Patrick had gone to high school together. She had been one of the prettiest girls in school at the time, and having aged well, was now one of the prettiest women in the area. "What are you doing here?"

"I came in to spend some time up at my cabin on top of Fork Mountain."

"How long will you be around?" she asked.

"For a while. I'm trying to get back up there before it gets dark though. I can come chat later. But did anyone bring a phone up here they found by the river? I was swimming down there earlier."

"No," she said. "If anyone around here found a cell phone at the river they probably kept it." This was not something Patrick wanted to hear.

"What about the girl that came up a few hours ago to get out of the rain?" Patrick asked. "She came up here to hang out on your porch under the roof."

"I've been up here all day and I haven't seen anyone," Nikki said, boredom thick in her voice. "We haven't had anyone here since last weekend."

"You didn't see anyone during the rain storm?" he asked.

"No," she said. "I even walked out there myself to watch it rain for a while."

"Ok," he said, frustrated. "Well if anyone does come up here with a phone can you hang on to it? I'll come by in a couple days and check again."

"Sure," Nikki said, before averting her attention back to her computer screen. Patrick glanced over and noticed that she was playing Farmville on Facebook. "It was great seeing you again," she added.

Patrick walked back down to the river, scanning its banks in the hopes of seeing Amy again. She was way too young for him as far as anything romantic went but he had enjoyed talking to her this afternoon. Not to mention the fact that she might have his cell phone.

Seeing that Amy nor anyone else was there he got in his big Dodge pick up and headed up Fork Mountain. He got there with plenty of daylight left. After getting out of his truck he was amazed at what was waiting for him on the small front porch. Laying there in front of the door was his cell phone and a pair of sunglasses. The very pair he hadn't even realized he had left behind with his phone.

"I need a beer," Patrick said to himself upon entering the cabin. "Where's that doll?"

He had moved Samantha's cabbage patch doll around several times in the last couple of days, always consciously aware of exactly where he left it.

"Okay," he said to the doll as it sat in the chair in the living room. "As long as that little thief doesn't take you. She can have all the trash and cookies she wants."

Patrick walked back outside and got his beer and the few food items he'd purchased that day out of the truck. He brought them in and loaded them in his cooler, though he had no ice, and walked back out to the porch. He still was not used to the serenity of the mountain top.

However, this was his new life on the mountain. A life he was going to have to struggle to accept. He had always enjoyed the peaceful, easy feeling of West Virginia in his youth, but his life in adulthood had been anything but.

The events of his day took on a whole new meaning. Sure, he wasn't signing any business contracts or moving up any corporate ladders, but he hoped those days were behind him now anyway. At least for a while.

He enjoyed his conversation again with Heather at the library and was looking forward to her and her son coming up on Saturday. It was wonderful seeing his sister again as well. He had enjoyed meeting Amy, as mysterious as she had been.

Had she really walked all the way up Fork Mountain to deliver his phone and sunglasses? He had not told her exactly where he was staying but he knew it wouldn't have been hard for anyone to figure out. Still, it was nearly a three mile walk, straight up hill. In his youth, during his high school and college track days, he could run three miles in just under sixteen minutes on a flat surface. With the mountain as steep as it was, it would take forty five minutes to traverse on foot even at a quick pace.

Why hadn't Amy hung around if she had come up the mountain? Where did she go when she left? Patrick thought to himself that he really would like to see her again. At least to confirm that it was her who brought his items back and thank her if it was. The scary thought however, was what if it hadn't been? That would mean someone was stalking him.

"That's crazy" he mumbled as he opened another beer, sitting back comfortably in a folding nylon chair, similar to the one he had seen Phillip Ables in that morning. His, however, had nice resting arms with drink holders.

That was an entire different subject; Phillip Ables, and all the things he had spoken of. Patrick was sure that spending all those years alone on this mountain, not to mention all that time in prison, would be enough to drive anyone crazy. There was no cable on this mountain, no internet. What would a person do to occupy their time? Patrick figured Phillip spent his time spying on whoever came up here and looking for ghosts.

"Ghosts!" Patrick laughed at the thought. If anything, he imagined if there were ghosts on this mountain they would be much older than the little girls he'd been seeing. He knew of the graves on the hill but they had to be at least two hundred years old. Maybe older. He doubted they had girl scouts back then. He thought that if he were to see any ghosts they would be adults from pre-civil war days. The most likely explanation of the graves was that they belonged to the first family that settled on the mountain.

He knew quite a bit about the history of the town. It had been built around the timber industry with the first major lumber mill, the Cherry River Boom and Lumber Company, coming to the area around the year 1900. Perhaps the graves belonged to a logging camp in those days or even before?

He wasn't surprised that no one really knew. Back in those days people usually raised their families, worked hard at some type of forest job, then buried their family members as they died off.

"I'll figure out who is in those graves," he decided. He still knew a few old timers around town. He would make it his goal to find the answers.

The sun began to set over the hill above Patrick's small piece of land. With the graves being on top of the hill, the sun would hit that part of the land last before dropping even further to the west. It was definitely a nice resting place for whoever was buried there. The area was so beautiful and peaceful.

Patrick's thoughts were interrupted by a loud crash in the woods just on the other side of the field. Before whatever it was that made the sound came out of the woods he found himself growing excited. He knew it was either a white tailed deer or a black bear coming out, just before dark, to feast on any apples that had fallen from the apple trees during the day. If it were indeed a bear, he knew that it might even climb into the trees to eat some that had not yet fallen. He used to love to sit up here with his father just before dark and witness such activity. It was something that he had always hoped he could someday share with Samantha. That day would never come.

Just a minute later, a black bear did indeed pop its head out of the undergrowth. It was one hundred yards away from Patrick. He wasn't scared. He had spent enough time on this mountain and with the wildlife to know that the bears, no matter how large, were more afraid of him than he was of them.

He watched as the bear whipped his nose around in the air, smelling to see if the coast was clear. Bears have good eyesight, but their sense of smell is even better. After taking a few whiffs, the bear looked directly at Patrick. Though he had remained motionless and silent the bear knew he was there. It stared at him for a few seconds then meandered into the field, going straight for the apple tree that was closest to it.

 Patrick watched in awe as the bear stood up on its hind legs, its front paws resting against the tree's trunk, and began eating the apples it could reach. The bear stood at least six feet tall. It ate only a few apples, then stared back at Patrick. It then made its way back into the woods the same way it had come out.

Patrick finished his beer then headed back inside. There would be more nightlife coming out to the field but it was growing too dark for him to see. He decided to knock off the drinking and get to bed. He had told his mother and sister that he could "control" his drinking, so he decided to do just that. At least tonight. Besides, part of this new life of his involved taking better care of himself, to include reducing the amount he drank, if not eliminating it all together.

Patrick spread his sleeping bag out on the couch in the living room. He didn't mind sleeping up stairs in the fall, but in the summer months, it seemed all the heat of the day made its way to the bedrooms and never dissipated until the wee hours of the morning.

Not being able to get comfortable because it had been an exceptionally hot day, and therefore translated into an exceptionally warm evening in his un-air conditioned cabin, he rose and walked over to the front door. He propped it open to allow a breeze to enter. He went to the back door and did the same.

"Better keep hold of you," he said to Samantha's doll, picking it up and clinging it to his chest like a child would a teddy bear. More so, just as Samantha had done with this very doll years ago.

#

Patrick sat in his nylon chair on the river bank. He was with Samantha, cat fishing on the banks of the Potomac just outside of Washington D.C. They rarely caught anything, other than the few sunfish that Samantha managed to catch on her Barbie fishing pole. She loved to catch them but always made her father take them off of the hook. She would always give them a little kiss on the mouth before throwing them back in the river. Her mother thought it was gross, but Patrick always considered it one of the cutest things he'd ever seen.

"Daddy! I have a big one!" She shouted.

"Reel it in honey."

"I can't, it's too strong," she said, the line squealing out of her reel.

"You can do it," he said, a smile on his face.

"This is your fault, Daddy," she said, just before being pulled in the water. She went head first, completely under, never to come up again.

#

"Samantha!" Patrick woke with a start.

Looking around he realized after a few seconds where he was. He was in his cabin on top of Fork Mountain. The sun was blaring into the window on the east side of the cabin.

"Morning already?" he mumbled to himself. Looking at his watch he realized it was seven thirty. "That was a quick night."

He rose to his feet. There was a late summer's morning chill in the cabin. He walked to the back door and shut it. He did the same with the front door of the cabin.

He was shaken from the dream. He sat down at the kitchen table and began to sob.

The Graves…

The words came as a whisper through the cabin.

"Who's there?" Patrick said, rising to his feet. "Is that you Trixie?"

He ran into the living room, from where he thought the voice had come. No one was there.

"I've been up here less than a week and I'm losing my mind," he said, rubbing tired eyes.

He made his way back to the kitchen, his mind still on the dream that had awakened him.

...of the babes

"Who's there!" he said, rising to his feet again. This time he went through the living room and peaked his head up the stairs. There was no one else in the cabin. He dropped to the floor of the living room and ran outside. He looked all around and no one was there either. He was convinced he was hearing voices.

"I didn't even get drunk last night," he said, walking back into the house.

If nothing else, thinking he had heard a voice for a second time took his mind off of his dream. He went to his cooler and pulled out the dozen eggs he had bought at the store the day before. He knew they would still be good but he also knew he would need to pick up some ice from the store while in town today. Better yet, he decided he would dig his old college dorm fridge out of his mother's storage. He would swing by the Lowes in Summersville, the next town over, and pick up a gasoline powered generator. He should have done this by now but better late than never.

He quickly made a ham and cheese omelet using his old Coleman gas stove top that was still in the cabin. He and his father had cooked plenty of meals with it during hunting seasons of years gone by. He ate with a vengeance, deciding he could definitely get used to solid foods.

The day was early and he decided to get some work done before heading off of the mountain for the few incidentals he needed. He made his way out to the old shed again and was happy to see the old riding mower still in good shape. There was a five gallon can half full of gas. He fueled up, backed out and began mowing the field. This would keep him busy until lunch time, and hopefully keep his mind off of Samantha.

Patrick found his mind filled with pleasant thoughts as he took wide turns around the field. He had set the blade at its highest level, about eight inches off the ground. He would need to mow at this level before coming through again, perhaps in a few days, to get a closer cut.

He made his way to the trail leading up to the graves and decided he would mow a path there as well. If nothing else this would make it easier for Phillip Ables to spy on him. Patrick had decided to flatter the old hillbilly until he reached a point of being obnoxious.

When he reached the top of the hill, he saw something that had gone missing the day before. The bag of trash the little girl had taken from his truck was laying on one of the graves. It had been ripped open, more than likely by a bear or raccoon, and several of the cans had been pulled out and kicked around.

Patrick got off the mower, gathered up the mess, put it in the storage area on the back of the mower then began to mow a path around the grave site. As he was nearly finished, his blade jammed, stalling the motor. He quickly killed the ignition and jumped off to see what he had caught, assuming it to be a stick or tree root.

Patrick lifted the mower up on its side a bit and saw that a piece of cloth was caught in the blade. He reached in and pulled it out. He examined it closely.

From what he could tell, it appeared to be a sash. It was dark green in color, about ten inches long and six inches wide. That is at least how much of it was sticking out of the ground. It probably had not originally been as light a shade of green as it now was. Who knew how long it had been here, exposed to the elements, bleached by the sun.

He put it down and rolled the mower forward. He went back to the cloth and gave it a hard tug, pulling it out of the ground along with a big clump of dirt and grass. A white larva of some sort wriggled angrily, having been not too happily disturbed.

The sash had several old patches on it, too worn for Patrick to make out.

"This must be Sarah's," he said. "How long has she been coming up here?"

He put the sash on the mower with the bag of trash. He would give it to Sarah if he ever saw her again. He mowed another path around the graves, more careful this time not to hit anything else. However, he hit a piece of trash, the blades shredding it and throwing it all over the place. He stopped again to pick up as much of it as he could.

A girl scout cookie box! How did this get up here? Had Trixie taken this too? He did find it in the same place he'd found the bag of trash that he saw her take. Why was she bringing what she stole from him up to the graves?

After cleaning up what he could of the cookie box he headed back off of the hill. He parked the mower in front of the cabin beside his truck and went in for a sandwich. He washed it down of course with a warm beer. He had gotten to where he preferred warm beer to cold water.

After his small lunch he made a list of things he would pick up while in Summersville. Sure, the bare necessities could be had in Richwood, but that was it. If one were in need of anything other than the bare essentials of sustaining themselves, they had to make the forty minute drive to the other side of the county.

He included on the list an outdoor shower bag, one that would hold five gallons of water. He and his father had used one years ago but he could not remember what had happened to it. If he were to spend considerable amounts of time up here, especially getting dirty and sweaty like today, he would need to be able to shower. He had enough scrap wood and paneling to build a stall like the one he and his father had used that had since decayed.

He made his way off the hill and less than an hour later was in Summersville picking up the few odds and ends he needed. He wasted no time in Lowes or anywhere else he went. He wanted to get back on the mountain.

As he rolled into Richwood however, he decided to go by and see one of the local living encyclopedias, Bill Hammonds.

8

Patrick rolled into the driveway of the small, clapboard sided house that sat just at the edge of town. It had been one of the town's original houses, built at the turn of the last century to house families working in the timber industry. A tall pine tree climbed high into the sky in the backyard, perhaps the only thing in the immediate area older than the house itself.

"Can I help ya?" the old man said when he answered the door.

"Hi," Patrick said. "We've never met, but I know you to be a legend as far as local history of the town goes. I was wondering if I could borrow some of your time to pick your brain?"

"Come on in," the old man said, turning to walk toward what was obviously his favorite chair, swatting an old cat out of it before it could get too comfortable. Patrick followed and took a seat in a similar chair across from him.

"My name is Pat Hanna," he introduced himself.

"Your dad worked over at the mill for a long time, didn't he?" Bill said. "I never met him but I know of him." He was giving Patrick proof that if there was anything to know about anything or anyone in Richwood, he was the one who would know it. "Sorry to hear of his passing a couple years back."

"Thanks," Pat said. "I've known who you are my entire life. You'll have to forgive me but when I was younger I never cared much about local history, but the older I get the more interesting it seems."

"Yeah," Bill chuckled. "That's just part of getting older. Seems like the further away the good old days get, the more we tend to miss them."

Bill would turn ninety one this fall. He didn't appear to be a day over seventy five. He had outlived his wife, four years his junior, as well as most of his friends. In spite of his age, he still lived alone and got along quite well.

"I am staying in our cabin up on top of Fork Mountain and I was wondering if you could tell me a little bit about the history of the place?"

Patrick was surveying his surroundings as he spoke. The room was filled with local history books. Bill had actually contributed to most of them. Any time anyone was writing a book not just on the local history, but also the history of timbering or the history of the state's railroads, mostly used for timbering, they called on Bill Hammonds.

Years before, when the government themselves were out of options while redoing the topography maps of the area, they had called on Bill for help. He was able to take their maps and fill in the remaining names of every stream, hollow, run or hill top in the area.

"I was born up one such holler, on the banks of the Williams river in 1919, while my parents were living in an old logging camp," Bill said.

His father had been a lumberjack and Bill himself would later spend nearly half a century working in the forests.

"What part of Fork Mountain's history do you want to know about?" Bill asked.

"There is a graveyard up there," Patrick said, sitting back, becoming more comfortable. "What can you tell me about it?"

"I can tell ya about the last man buried there," he said. "My grandfather was the clergyman overseeing the funeral."

"Is that right?" Patrick said, amazed and convinced he had come to the right place for answers.

"It was the spring of 1886," Bill began. "My grandfather had been a captain for the confederate army during the civil war. After the war, he became a circuit preacher."

"I've heard of those," Patrick said. "They covered quite a bit of territory didn't they?"

"They sure did," Bill agreed. "My grandfather covered this part of Nicholas county as well as Pocahontas and Greenbrier counties. He'd plant a garden in the spring, then take off on his route and return just in time for the harvest."

"Wow!" Patrick said, amazed. "He was gone that long?"

"Sure was," Bill said. "He used to take my dad with him. When he was eight years old my father was hiking through these trails around here, camping in the woods with his dad, until they reached their destination."

Bill settled back in his chair now, crossing his right foot across his left knee. He clasped his hands together, resting them on his lap. Patrick could tell he was entering reminiscence mode. The old man was about to tell him stories he hadn't come to hear, but stories to which he would be more than happy to listen.

"I remember walkin' through the woods with my dad when I was a kid back in the 1920's. He'd point to a rock overhang and say, 'see that,' and I'd say, 'yeah,' and he'd tell me he'd spent the night under there with his dad years ago."

"So they'd just walk all day then set up camp wherever they happened to be when the sun was going down?"

"Yeah," Bill said. "What ya gotta understand about those days though, is that there were usually other people out there in them woods. They'd have stone houses or small, wooden shanties. Most of 'em were loggers, some of 'em ran stills. They were good people nonetheless and they'd usually jump at the opportunity to feed a preacher dinner. Heck, many of 'em hadn't seen another person other than them they worked with in months. Dad said they always loved the company."

"Tell ya what would surprise ya if ya knew it," Bill said, coming out of his reminiscent trance, looking Patrick in the eyes. "They's lots of unmarked graves through all these hills."

"From lumberjacks dying out in the middle of nowhere?" Patrick asked, assumption in his tone.

"Well, that's one thing," Bill said. "Another is the fact that people used to just kill each other all the time back in those days. They could do it and get away with it, see. There weren't no law up all those hollers."

"Why would they kill each other?" Patrick asked.

"The two main reasons were women and dogs."

"Dogs?" Patrick said, amazed. "I can understand the women thing. Men have fought wars over women since the dawn of time, but dogs?"

"Oh yeah," Bill began. "You gotta remember. These old boys lived out in the mountains all alone. Dogs weren't just a man's best friend back then. Lots of times they were their only friends. If you were mean to a man's dog, especially if ya kicked him, why, that old boy would just pull out his gun and blow a hole through ya. He'd have ya buried within the hour and no one would even question your whereabouts for a year or more when ya didn't come out of the woods."

"So do you know where all these graves are?" Patrick asked.

"Some of 'em," Bill said. "My father would point some of 'em out to me when I was a kid. I doubt I'd ever be able to find 'em these days. I hadn't been up many of them hollers in seventy years."

"That time frame is too hard for me to even comprehend." Patrick said, feeling a deep sense of respect for the old man that sat across from him. "I can only imagine the changes you've seen around here in your lifetime."

"I've seen lots of 'em," Bill said. "I can remember when this town was boomin'. It was a boomin' from the 1920's through the 1950's. Why, we used to have the world's largest clothespin factory, the country's largest tannery and one of the country's biggest hub factories. They made wagon wheels. Anything that could be made out of wood was made here. Coal came next. We used to get more coal outta here than they do now in any other part of the state."

"So about the graves on Fork Mountain," Patrick said, bringing the matter of his visit back to hand. "What do you know about them?"

"Well," Bill began, drifting back into his previous state. "The winter of 1885/1886 was a bad one. There was a family living up there on top of the mountain and the old man of the house passed away. They'd usually just bury the bodies when that happened and wait for my grandfather to come through in the spring and hold the service. Well, the snow was so high and the ground was so frozen they couldn't dig a hole, so they actually left the body in the barn all winter till the thaw came. They buried him, then placed a big shale stone over the grave. My grandfather was up soon after and they had a real nice service for him."

"So, if they placed a stone over the grave, that means that it isn't even one of the graves that are noticeable," Patrick said. "I've counted eight and there may be more."

"Oh," Bill said, shifting nervously. "I can't tell you anything about those graves."

"Do you know about them?" Patrick asked, confused.

"You want a cup of coffee?" Bill asked, avoiding the question. "Are you in a hurry?"

"I'm not in a hurry," Patrick said. "I'll take a cup if you don't mind."

The old man gingerly got out of his chair and made his way to the kitchen.

"How do you take it?" he asked.

"Black," Patrick said.

The old man put a tea spoon full of Folgers instant in a mug and poured hot water from a teapot on top of it, allowing the water to mix it without needing to stir it.

"Here, now it's hot," Bill said, handing the mug to Patrick then returning to his chair. He had to nudge the cat out of it that had taken up residence the minute he had gotten up.

"Darn cat thinks this is his house, not mine."

Patrick sipped his steaming hot coffee. He didn't want to rush the old timer into telling a story he might not want to tell. He had respect for both the man's knowledge and age.

"Those graves were there long before my grandfather ever traveled that circuit," he finally spoke. "They've probably been there since we were part of Virginia. We didn't become an independent state until June of 1863 ya know?"

"Yeah," Patrick said. "I could tell that they are old. They are just marked with triangular shaped stones with no markings. They look like sinkholes facing east to west."

"Even when I was a young man, back in the forties and fifties it seemed no one could tell ya anything about those graves," Bill said.

"Someone it seems would know something?" Patrick pleaded.

"I have a friend that used to live up there," Bill said. "He's actually a couple years older than me. Still alive though. His name is Grady Haines."

"Would he know anything about them?" Patrick asked, taking a big swig of his coffee. It was cool enough to drink now without fear of burning his tongue.

"That man can't tell ya his own name," Bill said.

"Alzheimer's?"

"Insanity!" Bill snapped, causing Patrick to spill a bit of coffee from his mug. "He's been in an asylum for nearly sixty years."

"What happened?" Patrick asked, feeling nervousness rise in his chest.

"Don't know?" Bill said, more calm now. "He would go up on that mountain hunting and over time he started talking about hearing voices and all kinda crazy things. Said he was seeing Indian spirits or ghosts. Something like that. I don't remember the full story. All he seemed to be doing was scaring his younger sister who was living with him at the time. She eventually had him committed."

"That is strange," Patrick said.

"Even stranger, she ended up committing suicide herself a short time later. She ate a bullet from a .45 pistol."

Patrick took another swig of coffee to wet his throat. It had been getting dry, a result of nervousness.

"Both of them always had a troubled life," Bill added.

"How so?" Patrick asked.

"Their mother had actually killed their father and their uncle. Grady was just a boy and witnessed both murders. The woman was pregnant with Grady's little sister at the time so she never saw it."

"What on earth caused her to do that?" Patrick asked.

"The story goes that she was involved with her husband's brother. She figured killing her husband would get him out of the way. However, after she did, her lover cast her off so she killed him too."

"Did she go to prison?" Patrick asked.

"She never saw the inside of a jail cell."

"How is that possible?"

"All I know is that the judge at the time ended up owning two hundred acres of her land. He sold it off less than a year later at a handsome price. Just a good old fashioned, backwoods land deal I guess. The old lady gave up most of her land in exchange for her freedom. She had to move Grady and herself down off the hill and live in the hollow there below. That's where they were livin' when Grady's sister was born. Most people thought the girl was the child the other man."

"There have been a lot of strange things happen on that mountain then, haven't there?" Patrick said, taking another sip of coffee. It was doing nothing to wet his throat.

"There's been some stranger things than that happen up on that hill," Bill said. "I remember when I was a boy they found a man hanging from a noose in a tree up there."

"Did someone hang him?"

"They could never find no evidence as such so they wrote it off as suicide."

Patrick was growing more nervous by the minute. He had come here to get a history lesson and he felt as if he were listening to ghost stories. Maybe coming wasn't such a good idea. He wasn't getting the answers he was looking for. In fact, he was getting information he would have preferred not to get.

"Well," Patrick said, putting his empty mug on the coffee table. "I want to get back up there before dark. Thanks for your time but I'd better go."

"I'm not scarin' ya off, am I?" Bill asked, rising to his feet, his old cat jumping back into the chair as soon as he did.

"Oh no," Patrick assured him. "You're just answering the questions I've been asking."

"You take care up there," Bill said as Patrick made his way to the door.

"I will," Patrick said. "Thank you so much for your time. If I can think of any other questions I have I'll come back and see you."

"You're always welcome here, Pat."

Patrick got in his truck and began backing out of the driveway. He made his way to the road and headed back up toward the mountain.

Bill Hammonds made his way back to his seat, nudging his old cat out of it so he could sit again. He fumbled through a stack of old scrapbooks that were piled beside his chair. He took one up and opened it to a newspaper article he had cut out and filed in the scrapbook years ago and read the headline.

"Third Child Goes Missing on Fork Mountain."

The rest of the week passed quickly. Pat got a lot done at the cabin. He had set up the new generator he had purchased at Lowes and gotten electricity running in his cabin. He was now using his new dorm refrigerator to keep his beer and food cold. Now that he had a refrigerator he graduated from lunch meat only to other foods as well.

He had built a shower stall that he was now using daily. He had bought a new shower bag he hung in it that absorbed the sunlight, heating the water so that every evening he could take a warm shower after his day's labor. He had gotten the field mowed to an acceptable level and even managed to chop some firewood. He didn't know if he would be around for winter but he wanted to be prepared in case he was.

He had started sitting around a fire at the edge of the field in the evenings, just as he and his father had done years ago. He enjoyed listening to the owls sound off back and forth from mountain to mountain. On occasion he would hear turkeys cackling as they were roosting in trees for the evening above his cabin on the hill where the graves were located.

This morning, Saturday, he drove into town to meet Heather and Caleb. Though the road was acceptable for his truck, there was no way Heather could have gotten her car up the mountain.

"This is really nice up here," Heather said upon arriving at the cabin.

"Thanks," Patrick said. He was happy that she was impressed. He had worked so hard all week to make the place presentable, her visit in mind.

"I got a few steaks at the store yesterday," he said. "We can grill them outside and take in the scenery. It isn't that hot today."

"That's a great idea," she said. "It is so beautiful up here I wouldn't want to be inside."

While Patrick set up the grill, Heather walked with Caleb in the field. He got comfortable with a sizable area where there were no apple trees or other obstructions. He sat in the grass and breathed in the mountain air. Having assured his mother he would be ok, he played in the general vicinity while she made her way back to Patrick for conversation while he cooked.

"That sure is a special kid you have there," Patrick said when Heather returned.

"Yeah," she said in agreement. "I don't think I would want him any other way. I know it would be nice if he could see, but I think we are closer because he can't."

"That makes sense," Patrick said. "You've probably spent a lot of extra time with him that you wouldn't have if you didn't have to. I know I took a lot of time for granted with Samantha."

Patrick was surprised he had mentioned his daughter. Not so much because he never spoke of her, but because he felt as if he could do so now comfortably. He felt at ease around Heather. He always had.

"That is so terrible what happened, Pat," she said. "I can't imagine."

"Yeah," he said, flipping the steaks. "It just isn't fair ya know? And I'm not talking about me either. I'm talking about her. I'm an adult. I know that bad things happen in this world. But there are certain things a child should never have to experience."

"Yeah," Heather agreed. "Did anyone ever find out exactly what happened?"

"No," he said. "That is what makes it worse really. You don't know the thoughts that have gone through my head. All the possibilities."

Patrick fumbled with the tongs. He stopped talking and just stared into the charcoals.

"We don't have to talk about it, Pat," Heather said, noticing his pause.

"Oh, it's ok," he said. "You know I never do. I avoid it all the time. Maybe it would be good for me to get some of it out. I feel like I can talk to you about anything. I always have ya know?"

"I've always felt the same with you," she said. "Any time you need a friend you know how to reach me. You can call me any time or stop by. I love it up here. I wouldn't mind coming up again any time you are willing to have me."

"Don't tell me that," Patrick said, laughing. "I'll move you in by the end of the day."

Patrick pulled the steaks off of the grill, medium rare. Heather took notice that he had remembered how she liked her steak. It was always easy ordering when they had gone out for dinner years ago because of their similar tastes.

He had brought out some plates and utensils and set them on the picnic table in the yard. He and Heather looked out into the field at Caleb. She was about to get him and walk him over for lunch.

"Is he talking to himself again?" Heather said.

Patrick looked into the field and saw that Caleb was talking to Sarah. He had not even noticed that she had shown up. One minute she was not there and the next she was.

"Talking to himself?" Patrick said, wondering why Heather made no mention of Sarah.

"Yeah," Heather said, turning to face him. "Mrs. McClung, his teacher said he's been talking to an imaginary friend in school lately. Just in the past week or so."

"I remember Mrs. McClung," Patrick said. "Didn't we both have her in grade school?

"Yes," Heather confirmed. "She is still the great teacher she always was. She looks like she hasn't aged."

"So what do you think is up with the imaginary friend?" Patrick asked. He looked into the field again and saw that Sarah was heading toward the wood line. He looked curiously at Heather who still made no indication that she noticed the little girl.

"I asked him about it one day after school. He said it is a little girl named Sarah."

Heather began walking into the field for Caleb. Had Patrick heard her correctly? Did she say Caleb's imaginary friend was a girl named Sarah? Yet Sarah had just been here. She was now somewhere in the woods.

Heather and Caleb returned, hand in hand, and all three of them sat at the table. Heather began cutting Caleb's steak. Patrick had made a salad the day before that he had brought out to the table. He had also gone through the field that morning before leaving to get Heather and Caleb and rounded up some fresh apples that the deer and bears had not eaten the night before.

"Do you like it up here, Caleb?" Patrick asked.

"Yeah," the boy said. "I want to come back."

"You like it that much, huh?" Heather said, now cutting into her own steak.

"Yeah," Caleb said. "Sarah lives up here."

Heather looked slightly embarrassed. Patrick felt his heart jump.

"Who's Sarah?" Patrick asked before Heather could say anything.

"She's a girl that's been coming to see me at school," Caleb said. "She's a girl scout."

Patrick froze, his mouth stopping in mid chew.

"She's a girl scout, honey?" Heather said, looking at Patrick with a smirk on her face, hoping that he didn't think her son was blind AND crazy.

"Yeah," Caleb said. "She said she lives up here."

"Did she say where she lives?" Patrick asked.

"She said she lives on top of the hill."

"Did she say where on top of the hill?" Patrick asked.

Heather shot Patrick a look. It was a look that said, 'don't encourage him.'

"No," Caleb said. "Just that she lives on top of the hill."

"Pat and I had Mrs. McClung in school when we were your age," Heather said, changing the subject.

"You did?" Caleb said, astonished. "I didn't know she was that old."

"Your mom's not that old," Heather said.

"You're pretty old," Patrick said, teasing her.

Heather laughed it off and kept eating, as did Caleb. Patrick continued eating as well but he couldn't believe what he had just heard from Caleb. So he was not crazy. Nor was he the only one that had seen Sarah. The hermit on the other side of the mountain had seen her and now, Caleb, his friend's blind son was seeing her as well. A boy who couldn't even see anything. But why had Heather not seen her? She had just been here, talking to her son.

After they finished eating, Heather walked Caleb back to the center of the field where he had been playing. She returned and started helping Patrick clean up from lunch.

"I wonder if I should take him to a child psychologist or something," she said.

"No," Patrick said.

"Do you think it's a phase?" Heather asked. "Did Samantha go through that?"

"No," Patrick said. "I mean, no, I don't think it is a phase. Samantha had her imaginary friends from time to time."

"Why don't you think it is a phase then?" Heather asked, stopping what she was doing to look Patrick in the eye.

"Because I've seen Sarah too," he said, continuing to clean, fearing what would come next. Heather would now expect an explanation.

"What do you mean you've seen her too? There was nobody there."

"She was standing there in the field talking to Caleb," Patrick said. "And this isn't the first time I've seen her."

"Ok," Heather said. "You're making me nervous now. What is going on here?"

"If I knew I would tell you," Patrick said. "All I know is that I've seen Sarah. I've also seen a little girl named Trixie. She likes to take things that don't belong to her."

"Is it possible that you and my son have the same imaginary friends?" Heather asked, smiling, convinced Patrick was teasing her.

"I guess anything is possible," he said, giggling. He decided it would be best to change the subject while he had the opportunity. "Those apples weren't very good. I think I know why the critters left them."

"They're not much more than crab apples are they?" Heather said, now continuing to help Patrick clean. She was convinced Patrick was only kidding her. He must have been, the way he changed the conversation so nonchalantly.

The three of them spent the rest of the afternoon outside. It was a beautiful Indian summer day. A light breeze was blowing from the east, cooling their sweat, brought about by the humidity, providing for nature's best form of outdoor air conditioning.

"I guess you'd better get us off this mountain before dark," Heather said. "I still remember that night we were up on the hill, and now that there is a mysterious girl scout running around that everyone but me seems to be able to see, I don't want to be up here after dark."

"Ok," Patrick said. "Let's get off the hill then."

Patrick drove Heather and Caleb back to their house in Hospital Bottom. They parted cordially. No hugs or kisses. They agreed to get together on top of the mountain again. Then Patrick made his way back to the top of the hill, stopping only once to pick up a twelve pack of beer from Mountaineer Mart, one of only two convenient stores in town.

Once back on the hill, he got out his nylon folding chair, sat it up in the yard and opened a beer. It would still be an hour before dark. He wanted to reflect on his day.

He had really enjoyed Heather's visit. He could tell too that Caleb enjoyed being on the mountain. He liked the fact that he could offer the kid a place where he could play without fear of injury. Thinking even more on the subject, he was realizing just how much he missed being a parent. It was nice having a child around.

Detecting movement on the other side of the field, Patrick looked up and saw a little girl, one he had never seen, run around the side of the building where he kept his lawn mower and tools. After getting to the side of the building, she peaked around the edge, as if she was expecting someone to be behind her.

"Ready or not, here I come," he heard another child's voice say.

A few seconds later, Sarah came gallivanting out of the woods, still wearing her girl scout uniform. The girl behind the building ducked her head back around the corner so she wouldn't be seen.

Patrick watched in silence. Was he really seeing this? Or was he being visited by imaginary friends?

"Found ya!" Sarah yelled as she came around from the other side of the building. "You always hide in the same place, Amelia. That's not fair. It isn't any fun. I want to play hide and seek for real!"

"Sarah!" Patrick yelled.

"He can see us?" Amelia said to Sarah.

"Yeah," Sarah said. "He's nice. He bought some cookies from me. Come on."

Sarah grabbed Amelia by the hand and started leading her toward Patrick. Amelia was older than Sarah, thirteen probably, and was willing to let Sarah lead her. She was tall and skinny with long brown hair and big brown eyes. She had fair skin and Patrick could tell she would make a beautiful woman someday.

"What are you guys doing up here?" Patrick asked when the girls drew near.

"We're playing hide and seek," Sarah said. "This is Amelia."

"Hello, Amelia," Patrick said.

"Hello," she said with a curtsy. She was very well mannered.

"Were you up here earlier today?" Patrick asked. "Talking to a little boy named Caleb?"

"Yes," she said. "He's my friend. He told me that his mom is your girl friend."

"Oooh," the girls cooed to each other, smiles on their faces.

"Why couldn't Heather see you?" Patrick asked, ignoring their teasing.

"It is hard for people to see us if everything is right in their life," Amelia jumped in. "We like it when we run into people like you." Amelia leaned over to whisper in Patrick's ear now. "It gives me someone to talk to other than these kids."

"I am really confused as to what is going on here," Patrick said.

Just then, though it had been sunny and cloudless all day, the sky began to grow dark. The wind picked up and the tree tops began to sway. The wind, so forceful, sounded like an F-16 taking off from some distant runway.

"Come on Sarah!" Amelia said, taking the younger girl by the hand. "We have to get out of here!"

"Wait!" Patrick said, rising to his feet. "Where are you going?"

"We have to run!" Sarah said. "He's coming!"

"Who's coming?" Patrick asked.

It was too late. The girls had entered the woods and were out of site.

Just then the skies opened and rain began to fall hard. Patrick grabbed his chair and made his way to the roof covered porch. He didn't go in the house. Instead, he sat on the porch and watched the storm.

Patrick had always loved storms on the mountain. They always seemed so much more violent up here than they had in the city. There were no man made distractions to detract from their magnificence.

Almost as suddenly as the storm had started, it stopped. Pouring rain gave way to a light drizzled that lasted only a minute before giving way to no rain at all.

A light cloud of fog made its way down the hill above the cabin, settling on the far side of the field. As the fog began to dissipate, an image made its way into Patrick's view. It seemed to be standing in the middle of the fog.

It was an image of an old man. He was holding a bamboo cane, similar to the ones that were in the fallen shed on top of the hill. The figure stood, gazing at Patrick.

"Mr. Ables?" Patrick asked, voice loud, with a hint of curiosity.

Patrick made his way off the porch. He walked hesitantly, yet committed toward the figure. Halfway across the field the fog that had seemed to be dispersing thickened again. Patrick watched as the fog fully enveloped the figure.

He continued walking toward the fog. As he did so it began to disappear again. When he had reached where it had been, it was completely gone. As was the figure.

Patrick turned and started to make his way back to the cabin. A few paces into his journey he felt and heard something crunch under his foot. He bent down and saw perhaps the strangest creature he had ever seen. At least the strangest he had ever seen in West Virginia.

He had stepped on a crawfish. However, this was no ordinary crawfish. It was royal blue in color. Even stranger than that, there were no streams, lakes or ponds on top of this mountain. There were natural springs scattered around the area but none were here in the field.

Noticing movement out of the corner of his eyes, he glanced over and saw another such crawfish scurry down a hole. After it had made its way into the ground the hole itself seemed to close up, leaving no trace that it had ever been there at all.

Sunday came and went with no events. Patrick enjoyed the day on the mountain and had gone down to have dinner with Ginny in the evening. He had a pretty restful night. One without nightmares and one without visits from imaginary friends or child thieves. On Monday morning he decided over breakfast to get to the bottom of the events that had been taking place on his land.

#

"Ms. Hanna," his sister answered the phone in her office at Nicholas County High School.

"Elizabeth, it's me, Pat," he said. "I need a favor."

"Sure, what do you need? A job?"

"No," he said. "Not yet at least."

Patrick appreciated the fact that his kid sister was willing to help him get some semblance of a life back when he was ready to do so.

"I need you to do some research for me if you have time," he said.

"What kind of research?" she asked.

"You live in Summersville. That is the county seat. The courthouse is there."

"Uh, dah, I know that," she said, sarcasm in her voice.

"You always were the smart one," he said, equally sarcastic. "I need you to go to the courthouse and check on some land deeds."

"Are you buying a house?" she asked.

"No," he said. "It is for the land up here on Fork Mountain."

"Are you in a dispute with one of those holler people up there?"

"No," he said. "I love those people. They're harmless and I know that if anything ever happens up here they'd be able to tell me who exactly was up here and when. They're always watching."

"Then what's up?"

"I want to know who owned this land before the old man Dad bought it from did. I think the Smith's bought it back in the 1920's from the judge who owned it after the Haines family, but I don't know anything going back later than that. I'd like to know how far the records go back and what they say."

"Why?" she asked. The tone of her voice let Patrick know that she felt this task was of no importance, a waste of her time.

"You know there is that burial plot up here, right?"

"Yeah," she said, still not interested. "You and dad mentioned it to me years ago."

"Well, no one seems to know who is buried there or how long they've been buried. I talked to Bill Hammonds last week, the local historian, and he didn't know anything about it. He is almost ninety one years old. If he doesn't know, the only place we might be able to find anything out is at the courthouse."

"Ok," she said. "My planning period is actually the last hour of the day. I can leave early and go to the courthouse. I think they are open until five."

"That would be great," he said. "I'd really appreciate it."

"Ok," she said. "I just had a parent come in. I have to explain why it isn't the school system's fault that her kid acts like a jerk." She said this in a whisper.

"I understand," Patrick said, then hung up the phone.

He sat at the table weighing his options. He felt good knowing he had recruited the help of his sister. It would save him the long trip to the courthouse on the other side of the county.

As far as what he could do, he decided he could scour the internet for anything he could find. He would search for unmarked graves in West Virginia. He would search for online land records. He would leave no stone uncovered. If nothing else, it would give him more opportunities to see Heather at the library as well.

the graves...

Patrick froze when he heard the voice from what sounded like the other room. Had he really heard it?

...of the babes...

He decided he had indeed heard it. He didn't rise as forcefully as he had the last time he heard it. This time he decided to creep into the other room, look around the cabin.

He made his way first into the small, dimly light living room. Though he now had electricity no lights were on. He conserved gas for the generator as much as possible and rarely used it. Only at night or when he would have company.

He saw no one in the living room so he made his way upstairs. No one was there either.

He was convinced he was losing his mind. He had slacked up on his drinking a bit, at least over the past weekend, so he was not hung over or still drunk from the night before.

The strangest thing about the voice was that it was neither male or female. It sounded more like… air.

Thinking it must be a draft he checked to make sure the flew on the wood stove was closed. It was.

He went out on the front porch, just in time to catch a doe and her two fawns munching on some apples in the field. He sat in his chair and watched them eat. They fled just a few minutes later. He made his way into the house and grabbed a beer. He took it back outside and sat down in his chair to drink it. He had been working hard on not drinking in the mornings, but thinking he heard the voice again had rattled him. Alcohol had become his only means of coping.

"You're not going to find the answer you're looking for there," a voice came from the edge of the field, just behind him and to the right. He glanced around to see Amy, the girl he had met at the river, making her way to the porch.

"I'm glad to see you," he said. "I wanted to thank you for bringing my cell phone and sunglasses up here last week."

"You're welcome," she said, sitting down cross legged in the grass in front of the porch. Patrick couldn't help noticing her long, sinuous legs as she crossed them. Her shorts were very short in deed. He did the gentlemanly thing of not staring. He instead kept eye contact with her.

"Why do you drink so much?" she asked.

"It's just one beer," he said.

"It's only eight thirty in the morning," she said.

"Why are you up here so early?" he asked. "Why are you up here at all?"

"I like to walk in the mornings before it gets too hot," she said. "These hills give me a great workout without having to run."

"I like to drink in the mornings before it gets too hot," he mused. "Twelve ounce curls give me a great workout without having to lift weights."

"Fair enough," she snickered.

"Amy," he began. "What is going on up here?"

"What do you mean?" she asked. Patrick got the feeling she knew exactly what he meant but that she was making sure they were on the same page.

"This seems to be a pretty popular place, to be so secluded especially," he said. "You are not the only kid that I've been seeing up here."

"I'm nineteen!" she said, defensively.

"You know what I mean," he said.

"So who all have you seen?" she asked.

"I've seen you, Sarah, Amelia and Trixie."

"So how much stuff are you missing," she said, in reference to Trixie.

"So far all she's taken is a bag of garbage and a box of girl scout cookies. At least as far as I know."

"So you've seen us all have you?"

"Yes," he said. "I hope that is all of you. Are there more?"

"One other," she said. "I hope you don't see him."

"Who is he?"

"A very mean old man," she said, a chill running down her spine.

"You mean Phillip Ables?"

Amy got a warm smile on her face. Her eyes lit up like a kid on Christmas morning.

"Have you seen…" she paused, choosing her words wisely. "Have you seen Phillip?"

"Yeah, do you know him?"

"Yes," she said. "I know him but I've not been able to talk to him."

"He's up here all the time. I think he sits in a chair up on the hill and spies on me quite regularly."

"Will you tell him that I said hello?" she said.

"Sure," he said. "Anything else you want me to tell him?"

"Yes," she said, again pausing as if choosing her words carefully. "Will you tell him that I know he didn't do those terrible things he was accused of doing?"

"Sure," he said. "How do you know that though? How do you even know about it at all?"

"Everyone from around here knows about that," she said, offering nothing more.

"Didn't you tell me you were just passing through when we met?" he said, remembering their previous and up until now, only conversation.

"You have a good memory," she said. "I didn't tell you from where though. People all around knew about that when it happened. It was a pretty big deal."

"So just where are you from, Amy?" he said. He found Amy to be quite mysterious. "And all those things happened before my time. I'm nearly twice your age."

"I'm from here, there and everywhere," she giggled. "I like to remain mysterious."

Patrick wondered if she was reading his mind. There was no way she could be. It just wasn't possible. Or was it?

Amy stood up, uncomfortable now that the conversation had made its way to her. She brushed off her shorts and began walking away.

"I want to finish my walk before it gets too humid," she said. "Please make sure you tell Phillip what I said. And don't forget your stuff the next time you're swimming. That hill is steep."

"Ok," Patrick said, rising to his feet. "You don't have to go you know."

"Yes I do," she said. "It will be hot soon."

"Come back anytime," he said, wondering why he hadn't made the same offer to his other visitors. Perhaps it was her legs and her age. It was definitely her legs and her age.

"Oh, I will," she said. With that she was back on the trail that passed for a road, making her way off the mountain. At least she appeared to be making her way off the mountain.

\#

An hour later Patrick was at the library doing research. It turned out that it was Heather's day off. He had hoped to see her, but didn't mind as much because now he had an excuse to call her. Not that he needed one.

Without her here to distract him however, no fault of her own, he was able to dive right into his research. He powered up his lap top, got online and started googling everything he could think of.

A search for unmarked graves in West Virginia took him to several not for profit groups that made it their mission to protect such sites. He scoured the lists of grave sites they provided on their sites but could find nothing on the Fork Mountain area outside of Richwood. The closest he came was to an unmarked grave beside the grave of legendary, female civil war spy, Nancy Heart. She was buried up Greenbrier Road on another mountain top overlooking Richwood. There was an unmarked grave beside hers, but it turned out that it belonged to a gentleman who used to man the fire tower at that location. He would spend days, as a livelihood, watching out for forest fires. He thought the area so beautiful that he had requested to be buried there when he died.

He found lengthy articles pertaining to the burial practices of the puritans, many of whom had spread west from Jamestown, Virginia through the mid 1600's. It was common for them not to carve memorials in the head stones of their grave markers due to their beliefs against "graven images." They wanted to honor God in death, not the dead themselves. This could be a possibility.

There were more articles still, pertaining to the practice of civil war soldiers often burying their dead comrades in unmarked graves, in the hopes of some day returning to reclaim their bodies.

Patrick didn't think this would be an option. Bill Hammonds' grandfather had been a Captain in the confederate army during the civil war. Had the graves belonged to soldiers, he was certain the older Hammonds would have known and passed that story down verbally.

"Maybe it is just puritans?" Patrick mumbled, fumbling with his searches.

He then decided to be a bit macabre. He started searching for unsolved murders or other mysteries that may have taken place in the area. His results were turning up nothing.

"What ya up to Pat?" Shelia, the librarian on duty today asked from behind. She was in her mid sixties. Patrick had remembered her as the librarian here when he was a kid.

"Oh, I'm just trying to find out any information I can on the land my cabin is on up on Fork Mountain."

"Most of that stuff, if any of it exists is not going to be online," Sheila said. "It was always stored on microfilm and most of it was never transferred over electronically when the internet came out."

"I never thought of that," he said.

"Why would you?" she asked. "You've had the luxury of growing up during the technological revolution. I bet you wouldn't even know how to look for stuff like that," she said with a giggle.

"Oh, you're right," he said. "I remember using it one time in sixth grade for a book report. It seemed like such a mundane practice that I learned to start paying girls to do my book reports for me in middle school. I had the feeling something would come along and replace the technology. I'm glad it did."

"Well," Shelia began. "I would be more than happy to show you were the microfilm is kept and how to use the reader."

"I would really appreciate that, Shelia."

"Too bad Heather isn't here to show you," she said, winking. News spread fast in a small town.

"If she were, I'd probably not get anything done," he laughed.

A few minutes later Sheila was showing Patrick how to load the thin strips of microfilm into the reader. It was a large, gaudy piece of equipment. A huge magnifying lens that resembled a periscope on a submarine was on top. Patrick put his face up to it and began reading the strip Sheila had loaded. It was the local newspaper, the News Leader, no longer in print, from 1980.

"The file there is full of every weekly issue going back to the 1940's," she said. "If you need any more help just yell for me."

"Ok, I will Sheila. Thanks."

Patrick was so caught up in his research that he worked straight through lunch. Time was flying by so quickly it was soon mid afternoon before Patrick began finding some articles of interest.

#

Third Child Goes Missing on Fork Mountain

July 28, 1971

A third child has been reported missing in the Fork Mountain area above Richwood, WV. The little girl, 10 year old Sarah Whitlock, was last seen by the local Girl Scout Den mother while picnicking with the group at the mouth of the Fork Mountain Trail above the first bridge on the North Fork of the Cherry River.

#

Patrick sat back quickly from the lens as if he'd seen a ghost! Perhaps he had.

"Oh my God," he whispered, before leaning back over to read the rest of the article.

#

The Richwood Fire Department, the West Virginia State Police, and the local National Guard unit scoured the woods for forty eight hours, day and night, in search of Whitlock with no success. Any information on the disappearance of the young girl scout should be reported immediately to local law enforcement. Sarah is four feet, eight inches tall and weighs seventy pounds. She has long brown hair and brown eyes.

#

Patrick sat back again. He could not believe what he had just read. His heart began to pound as if he were walking up Fork

Mountain, not reading about events that had taken place there.

Thoughts rushed through his mind. He no longer believed he was crazy or that alcohol was to blame for his visions. He was convinced now that it was no longer just his imagination playing tricks on him. This was reality! Sarah, among others, had come back from the grave. For some reason, they were visiting him. They had befriended him.

He spent the rest of the afternoon scouring more articles. It wasn't long before he found a similar article from three years before.

#

Local Girl Goes Missing in Richwood

April 4, 1969

Thirteen year old Amelia Hamrick was reported missing last week by her parents. The Hamrick family resides in the Weber City neighborhood of Richwood, WV at the foot of Fork Mountain.

A search conducted by many local agencies, to include the National Guard, overseen by the State Police, returned no evidence.

Amelia Hamrick is approximately five feet, two inches tall. She is lanky, weighing only eighty five pounds. She has long, straight brown hair and brown eyes.

Any information on the whereabouts or disappearance of Hamrick should be reported immediately. Local churches have pooled together a $10,000.00 reward for information leading to the discovery of the girl.

#

   Patrick continued searching. He was hot on the trail. He was not going to leave and come back tomorrow. His growling stomach now let him know that he had missed lunch. He looked at his watch. It was 3:30 p.m. He would work till dinner, until the library closed at 5:00.

Less than half an hour later he found what he was looking for again.

#

Local Child Missing in Woods in Fork Mountain Area

October 23, 1966

Eight year old Trixie Bennett has gone missing in Richwood, WV. The young girl and her friends were playing hide and seek in the woods behind her house in the Johnstown neighborhood of Richwood, at the foot of Fork Mountain. A thorough search by local authorities and volunteers has turned up nothing.

Trixie is four feet, six inches tall and weighs sixty pounds. She has curly, shoulder length, brown hair and brown eyes. Any information in regard to the disappearance or location of Trixie should be reported immediately.

\#

Patrick could not believe what he had found. He was absolutely dumb founded.

What about Amy? Was she part of this mystery? Had she gone missing as well? If so, when? If she had gone missing before the other girls, then Sarah would have been listed as the "fourth" girl to go missing. Had she gone missing later though, Patrick was sure he would remember hearing about it during his childhood.

Sarah went missing the year before he was born. Had Amy gone missing later, for sure in the small town of Richwood, there would have been such a stir that he would have heard about it. She had to have gone missing before. Maybe so much longer before that the authorities simply didn't include her in their count.

"We're closing up in a few minutes, Pat," Shelia said politely as she passed by, placing returned books back on the shelves.

"Ok," he said. "Just a few more minutes."

Knowing his time was now very limited, he chose to jump back a generation. He pulled microfilm from the cabinet drawers from the 1940's. Sure, he could always come back tomorrow, but he knew this mystery would keep him up all night.

He scrolled and scrolled, yet found nothing. No murders, no disappearances, nothing. Then, just as he was about to give up hope, an article jumped out at him.

#

Local Man Committed for Insanity

August 18, 1945

Grady Haines, a Richwood man, was committed to the Trans Alleghany Lunatic Asylum in Weston, WV last week by his sister, Linda. Haines, who resided up Handle Factory Hollow on Fork Mountain had been acting strange for some time according to his friends and relatives.

Haines spoke of battles with Indians, a Shaman, murder and other forms of nonsense. Fearing he was either participating in witchcraft, devil worship or that he in some way may pose a danger to himself or others, his younger sister thought it would be best to have him committed.

Visitors are welcome at the Asylum Monday through Friday from 1:00 p.m. to 5:00 p.m. During other hours, the best doctors in the land feel that shock treatment can rid Mr. Haines of his insanity, allowing him to return to his home on Fork Mountain.

#

This was the man that Bill Hammonds had mentioned briefly when Patrick had met with him. Perhaps Hammonds was not the man that Patrick should be talking to. Perhaps he should pay Mr. Haines a visit. Bill Hammonds had said the man was still alive. Now all Patrick had to do was find him. Land deeds and graveyards would now take a back seat in his investigation. Patrick Hannah's number one priority was to find

Grady Haines. His time was limited. Hammonds had said Haines was older than he was. Patrick had no time to lose.

11

As Patrick was leaving the library, on his way to have dinner with his mother, Heather and Caleb were finishing up their dinner on the other side of town.

"Can I ask you some questions about your friend Sarah, honey?" Heather said.

"Yeah," Caleb said, guiding peas onto his spoon with his little fingers.

"Do you know that no one else sees her?" she asked.

"Pat can see her," he said, chewing.

"How do you know that?"

"Sarah told me."

"When did she tell you that, Honey?"

"Today," he said.

"So you saw her again today?" Heather asked, now more concerned.

"Yeah," he said. "She wanted to know when we were coming back to her place to play."

"What did you tell her?" Heather asked, concern evident in her voice.

"I told her it depended on when you wanted to go back up and see your boyfriend."

"Pat's not my boyfriend," Heather said. "We went to school together. He used to be my boyfriend. That was a long time ago though."

"I'm blind mommy, but I'm not dumb," he said, looking in her direction, though he couldn't see her.

"Why does she want you to go back up?" she asked, ignoring his remarks.

"She said she gets tired of playing with the same kids over and over," Caleb said. "She said she likes it when new people can see her. She said that not many can and that they usually get scared when they do."

"Why would they be scared of a little girl?" Heather asked.

"Because she's a ghost."

Heather almost choked. She had been grazing on what was left on her plate, not really eating in big bites now that she was full. She quickly grabbed her glass of water to take a drink, then coughed lightly to clear her throat.

"Do you believe in ghosts, Mommy?"

"Not really," she said. "But I guess anything is possible."

"When can we go back up to Pat's?" Caleb asked.

"I don't know, Honey. We'll have to see when he asks us up again. I haven't heard from him since this weekend but I'll probably see him at the library this week."

Heather got up and started clearing off the table. She couldn't believe what her son had just told her. She was thinking back now on how Pat had told her that he too had seen Sarah. If this was real, why hadn't she seen her? She had been there at the same time. She was hoping that Pat would indeed come into the library later in the week. If he didn't she would definitely give him a call.

#

"You just comin' down off the hill?" Ginny asked as Patrick walked in the door.

"No," he said, pulling the door shut behind him. "I've been at the library all day."

"Awe," she said, drawing the word out, smiling. "You've been hanging out with Heather?"

"No," he said, almost defensively. "She had the day off. I've been doing some research."

"What kind of research?" she asked.

"We can talk about it over dinner," he said, head motioning toward the kitchen. "I haven't eaten since breakfast and I smell something simmering in there. What is it?"

"I made some spaghetti. You're just in time."

The two of them made their way into the kitchen. Minutes later they were sitting at the table wrapping spaghetti around their forks.

"I had originally gone down to research land deeds," he said, shoving a big wad of spaghetti in his mouth. He chewed vigorously and swallowed before speaking again.

"But my search, when I found nothing, ended up taking quite an interesting turn." He shoved more spaghetti in his mouth and began to chew.

"Well, what did you find?" Ginny asked, shoving spaghetti in her mouth now as well.

"I found a lot of old articles on micro film about little girls that had gone missing back in the 60's and early 70's. Do you remember anything about that?"

"A little," Ginny said. "We had just come to town in 1972 when your dad got transferred to this mill. It was just in time because you were born the next year and I wouldn't have wanted to have had to move with a baby."

"What do you remember?" Patrick asked, still shoving spaghetti in his mouth. He was very hungry.

Ginny remembered Patrick having told her that a girl scout had come to his cabin to sell him cookies the morning after the first night he had stayed on the hill. She was wondering if his curiosity had anything to do with that. She wondered also if other strange things had taken place on the mountain top that he simply hadn't mentioned.

"We got here around the time it happened," she said. "I can't remember if it was right before or right after, but it was all the town talked about."

"Do you remember hearing anything about a couple other girls that went missing a few years before that?"

"Yeah," she said. "People around here were talking about that as well when the girl scout went missing."

"So you do remember that it was a girl scout?" Patrick asked, impressed with her memory.

"Oh yes," she said. "I never told you kids, but that is the reason I wanted to be the den mother when Elizabeth joined the girl scouts. By the time she joined, many years had passed, but as a parent you never forget those things."

"I know," Patrick said, thinking of Samantha.

"I don't know much about the other girls," his mother said, deciding to get his mind off of Samantha as quick as she could. "I always worried a little when you yourself played around in those woods. I didn't say anything to you, because the general consensus was that it was a serial killer. All the girls shared common traits. They were all brunettes with brown eyes. Whoever it was had probably moved on by the time you were a kid or had died."

She forked more spaghetti into her mouth. She chewed slowly, thinking, before speaking again.

"You know, they locked up that old hermit up there in the pen for twenty years. The conviction was based on circumstantial evidence. It was mostly based on the word of his brother, of all people. They never found any bodies. But the disappearances stopped once he was out of the picture."

Patrick and his mother ate in silence for a few minutes, both of them thinking.

"You know, that old hermit's family went through a lot there for a couple of years," Ginny finally spoke.

"How so?" Patrick asked.

"Well, just a few years before he was to get out of prison, his only child, a daughter, drowned up there at Rudolph Falls."

Now Patrick was choking on his food. He had to take a huge swig of water while his mouth was still full.

"You don't remember her name do you?" he asked when he caught his breath.

"No," Ginny said. "She was a beautiful girl. I don't think she was twenty yet."

Patrick was aghast. He had gone in the wrong direction while researching the microfilm at the library. He was now starting to remember the incident himself. For the longest time, he was not allowed to go swimming by himself at the falls. His mother or father, or a friend's parent was always with them.

"No, I take that back," Ginny said. "Her name was Amy."

Patrick froze, his mouth half full of water and half full of spaghetti. He simply stared across the table at his mother.

"What's wrong?" Ginny asked. "You look like you've seen a ghost?"

"I might have," he said.

"What are you talking about?"

"Oh, nothing," he said, deciding it would be best not to let his mother in on everything that had been going on on top of Fork Mountain. It is said that a mother always knows, but Patrick thought it best that his mother didn't know about these things.

\#

After dinner and more small talk with his mother Patrick made his way back up the mountain. As he was walking in the door, his cell phone rang. He would have ordinarily been amazed that he had reception up here, had he not worked for a cell phone company all those years and known just how powerful the signals could be.

"Hello?" he said.

"Hey Pat, it's Elizabeth."

"Oh hey, did you find anything out?"

"A little," Elizabeth said. "Before the judge got the land from the Haines' they had bought it from the Rogers' back in 1908. The Rogers bought it from the Spencers back in 1892."

"Wow, that's going back quite a way," Patrick said, impressed with his sister's work. He had known she didn't really want to do it but was happy that she had.

"The trail goes cold there Pat," Elizabeth continued. "I talked to the county clerk and she told me that more than likely the Spencers owned it at the time that West Virginia became a state in 1863. She said that for any information going back before then, if any existed, that we'd have to check the courthouse in Richmond, Virginia. I guess Virginia didn't transfer all the records over when the states split."

"So when are you going to Richmond?" Patrick mused.

"Ah, never," she said. "Unless you want to take me to Bush Gardens."

"As fun as that sounds," Patrick began, "I think I'll pass. I don't need to know now anyway."

"I wish you would have let me know that before I spent all afternoon at the courthouse."

"Well, I have another project for you," he said, ignoring her last statement.

"Great, what now?"

"I need you to find someone. A ninety three year old man named Grady Haines."

"Who's Grady Haines?" she asked.

"Some old man who lived on Fork Mountain in the 1940's. Supposedly he went crazy and his sister had him committed. I believe at the Trans Allegheny Lunatic Asylum in Weston."

"That place is a museum now," she said. "It was the state's mental hospital until Reagan threw all those people on the street in the 1980's. It sat empty for years, falling apart until some eccentric rich dude bought it and turned it into a museum. They have guided ghost tours there on Halloween."

"Well I know the guy is still alive," Patrick said. "I talked to one of his old friends last week who told me so. They had to have moved him. We need to find out where he is."

"What's going on Pat?" Elizabeth finally asked. "Why do you need to know all this information? Is something going on I should know about?"

"Nor really," Pat said. "I'm just trying to understand the history of this place."

"I'll do what I can, but I don't even know where to begin to find information like that."

"You'll figure it out," he said. "Like I said this morning. You always were the smart one."

"Oh brother! Literally!" Elizabeth said before hanging up the phone.

Patrick chuckled as he turned around. He stopped laughing though when he saw Trixie standing in the door. He had not shut it when he came in. She was standing there, an "I'm up to no good" smirk on her face. She was holding Samantha's doll.

"No Trixie," he said. "Anything but that. You can have anything you want except that!"

Trixie turned and sprinted out the door, the doll waving through the air, swinging in her hand as she ran.

Patrick took up the chase. He ran out the door, leaving it open behind him. He saw Trixie crossing the field into the woods, heading up the hill. Only half way across the field his heart was already pounding as if it were going to jump out of his chest. He made a mental note to start exercising.

Trixie was now in the woods. He could no longer see her but he had reason to believe he knew where she was going. Straight to the graves. She had gone in that direction and that is where he had found evidence of everything else she had taken from him.

Tree limbs slapped him in the face as he entered the woods. An unearthed root from a mature oak tree caught his foot and threw him to the ground.

"Ouch!" He got back up and continued running.

The hill was so steep that even if he were in better shape he would not be able to run up it. He slowed to a walk. Grabbing his knees with his hands forced himself up the hill. He knew his time to catch Trixie and get Samantha's doll back was growing short. It was growing dark quickly. The forest's thick canopy didn't help.

At the top of the hill and almost to the graves he could go no further. His lack of fitness and his age had caught up to him. He had to stop, catch his breath. For just a second he thought he might throw up.

Panting heavily, he felt his heart rate slowing. Sweat was dripping down his face. His shirt was soaking wet. It was still humid for this time of year and the run hadn't helped. He burped up a bit of spaghetti and immediately spat it out.

"Patty cake, patty cake, baker's man. Bake me a cake as fast as you can."

He heard the voice just above him. Obviously Trixie had thought he would not find her. She thought she was safe and was playing with the doll. Patrick decided it would be best to try to sneak up on her as quietly as possible.

"Roll it, and stuff it, and mark it with a B. Put it in the oven for Baby and me."

"Trixie?" Patrick said when he was only ten yards away, coming up from behind her.

"No!" she said defensively, pulling the doll tightly into her chest. She turned to face him.

"Look," he said, in between gasps for air. He was still very winded. "We can work something out, ok? You can come to my house and play with the doll any time you want. But I can't let you keep it."

"My doll," Trixie said, giving him her best mean look. Patrick just smiled. He thought she was cute.

"That belonged to my daughter," he said.

"I thought you said you didn't have any kids?" Sarah said, now coming out from behind a large poplar tree just behind Trixie. Amelia stepped out next. Patrick had not seen them. It was as if they had magically appeared.

"I don't," Patrick said. "I mean, I used to. She's dead now… I think."

"That's why you can see us," Sarah said, walking toward him, Amelia beside her. "You're broken."

"I'm not broken," Patrick said, taking a seat so Trixie wouldn't run again and because his legs felt as if they were going to fall out from under him if he didn't. "I have been getting along fine."

Shaking her head as if to say 'no,' Sarah walked within two feet of him. "No you're not, "she said. "I see you drinking beer all the time. If you were fine you wouldn't be sensitive enough to see us."

"You haven't let go yet," Amelia added.

"How can I?" Patrick asked.

"You just have to," Sarah said.

"Trixie," he said, now looking at the only girl who had not drawn close to him. He was certain it was because she was afraid he'd take the doll. "What do you say? You can play with her in the cabin. All three of you," he said, now addressing all of them, "are welcome to play in my cabin any time you like."

Just then the skies clapped with thunder and lightning. It had not been cloudy all day. Brilliant blue crayfish began popping up out of small holes that seemed to just appear on the ground.

Patrick thought it nothing more than a cloud burst, common in the mountains of West Virginia. It would often rain hard up one hollow or on a particular mountain top, yet nowhere else in the surrounding area. He remembered as a child walking to where the north fork and south fork of the Cherry River came together to see that one was flooding with muddy water from a storm somewhere up river, while the other fork was completely dry. He could not explain the blue crabs, however.

"Run!" Amelia said, grabbing Sarah by the hand, taking off through the woods.

"It's just a thunderstorm," Patrick said, rising to his feet.

"You can have your stupid doll!" Trixie said, dropping the doll at his feet, running by him in chase of the others.

"Girls!" Patrick yelled through cupped hands. It was too late. They were out of site.

He bent over and picked up Samantha's doll. He rose and turned back toward the graves just in time for the next brilliant streak of lightning. It revealed an old man standing over the graves, bamboo cane rod in hand. But just for a second. Just as quickly as the lightning had come and lit the world, all was black now that it was gone. Night had fallen.

"Mr. Ables?" Patrick asked.

"Outta my way!" the man said as he pushed Patrick to the ground and took up chase after the girls.

"What the…" Patrick said, rising to his feet, taking up the doll he had dropped on his way to the ground.

He too followed suit. The girls had run down the hill, in the direction of his cabin. He assumed the figure, who he thought was Phillip Ables, ran the same way. He made his way down the hill as quickly as he could, being cautious of protruding tree roots this time. The rain was coming hard, the occasional flash of lightning and clap of thunder, both lighting his way and exploding in his ears. Though being as careful as he could while running at such a quick pace he fell twice before making it to the field at the bottom of the hill.

As he entered the field, picking up speed now, lightning struck once again. This time he could see the girls running into his cabin. The man he believed to be Phillip Ables was halfway across the field in hot pursuit.

"What's going on!" Patrick yelled into the cabin when he entered, both rain and sweat dripping from his hair.

"Shhhh," Amelia said lightly, putting a finger to her lips. She was hiding behind the couch. Sarah and Trixie stuck their little heads out from the other side and pointed toward the ceiling, their heads motioning as well.

"He's up stairs?" Patrick asked.

All three girls shook their heads up and down in agreement. They seemed too terrified to make a sound.

"I'll take care of this," Patrick said, voice full of bravado. He dropped the wet doll on the couch then made his way over to the ladder and started up.

As he stuck his head up through the hold to the second floor, he let out a groan as something or someone grabbed him by the hair and pulled him the rest of the way up.

"You need to mind your own business," the man said, punching Patrick in the stomach. Patrick doubled over, holding his gut, sucking for air.

An uppercut came next, landing on Patrick's chin, throwing him to the ground. He almost fell back down the hole he had just come up.

The figure then began beating Patrick with the bamboo cane pole he had in his hand. Patrick suffered two hard blows before he finally caught it on the third strike. He wrestled forcefully, trying to take it from the man's hands.

"What are you doing, Phillip?" Patrick pleaded.

The figure let out a loud, eerie cackle. "I'm not that half sack Phillip!"

The fight continued. Patrick was unsuccessful in taking the stick. He did manage, however, to get out of the way of its next blow. He rolled on the floor, away from the hole that would certainly cause great bodily harm to him if he were to fall through it to the first floor below. He was able to get to his feet just in time to receive a bamboo cane rod blow across the face.

Patrick had decided he had had enough. He dove into the man, taking him to the floor. He threw a straight right that connected with the man's chin.

The blow should have knocked him out. At the man's apparent age, it should have killed him. It didn't even phase him. He laughed at Patrick instead. He laughed right in his face.

Patrick pulled back and swung again. This time the man must have moved because Pat hit nothing but the floor. Old, very hard, white oak floor.

"Awe!" Patrick let out a scream from the pain. He didn't dwell on it though because the man was gone. He jumped to his feet and looked around the room.

The next streak of lighting revealed the man, his back to Patrick, at the small window, looking out over the field.

"Darn it!" the man said. "They got away."

He had seen during the lightning strike that the girls were crossing the field and heading back into the woods. They were going the opposite direction of the graves. He knew he'd never find them tonight.

"Who are you and why are you tormenting those children?" Patrick asked, holding his throbbing right hand in his left. He was hoping for dialogue instead of continued violence.

The man turned to face him. The lightning revealed him with a smirk. However, he did not answer. He said nothing.

Patrick, still in pain, tried catching his breath. He had not had a good night so far.

Lightning stuck again. This time, it revealed that the man was gone. Almost as if he had vanished into thin air. Patrick had not heard him go down the stairs. He had not sensed him move. Just one second he was there and then he was gone.

The storm was gone as well now. As instantly as it had come it also disappeared. Just like last time. Thinking on that, he now realized this was the man he had seen in the fog, not Phillip.

Patrick fumbled his way down stairs. He immediately went to the front door. He shut and locked it. He then went into the kitchen. He had no ice for his hand, so he pulled out four cans of cold beer, put them in a plastic bag and placed his hand in the bag, two beer cans on each side. Just before sitting down, he thought better of it. He opened his small fridge again and pulled out a fifth beer. This one was for drinking.

"What in the world just happened?" Patrick said aloud as he popped the top. He took a violet swig, drinking half the can's contents in one drink. He could taste blood mixed with the beer. He realized his mouth was bleeding from the blow of the bamboo cane.

Patrick calmed down as his heart rate and adrenaline dropped. He was no longer breathing hard. After finishing his beer, which didn't take long, he took one out of the bag and began drinking it. His adrenaline surge now gone, he was too exhausted to rise to his feet and get one from the fridge.

His instincts told him to get off of the mountain. He knew he should go to his mother's or drive himself to the hospital. What would he tell his mother or a doctor had happened? He got into a fight with an old man who was trying to abuse some ghosts? That the old man was probably a ghost himself?

He had to come up with a story. He was sure he was going to be black and blue in the morning. He was sure he had broken his hand. What he wasn't sure of was whether or not he would be visited again tonight. He could stand a visit from the girls, especially if they came seeking protection. He just hoped that the man didn't come back. Not tonight. Not ever.

Patrick rose to go to the couch. He was not going to go back upstairs tonight. Before he left the kitchen he grabbed his box of beer from the fridge. Even if it got warm while he drank he wouldn't mind. He would rather drink warm beer than go back and forth to the kitchen. He was going to plop on the couch and remain there until morning.

"Just me and you tonight," he said to Samantha's doll. "I hope."

13

"Hello, my name is Elizabeth Hannah. I'm trying to locate someone who used to be a patient at the hospital," Elizabeth said to the lady who had answered the phone at Weston State Hospital. It was a newer facility on the other side of the small town of Weston, West Virginia from where the Trans Allegheny Lunatic Asylum had been. Obviously the name of the new facility was more politically correct in modern times.

"What's the name?" the lady on the other end of the phone said. Her voice let Elizabeth know that she wasn't any more excited about trying to be helpful than she was about helping Patrick.

"Grady Haines," Elizabeth said, rolling her eyes, hoping it didn't come through in her voice. She knew it didn't. This was common for her while dealing with parents. She had gotten good at it.

"The mom's on meth, the dad's in jail, and it's all the school system's fault," she would often say to friends, relaying the opinion of many of the parents she had to deal with.

"No records on a Grady Haines," the lady said.

"Where could I get a hold of the records of patients who were released in the 1980's under Reagan's 'let the nuts out on the street,' program?"

"What?" For the first time the lady on the other end of the phone showed signs of life.

"Never mind," Elizabeth said before hanging up the phone.

"Why did I let him talk me into this?" she asked herself, trying to figure out who to call next. Just at that moment, her phone rang.

"Hey Pat," she said, recognizing the number.

"Are you on your planning period?" he asked.

"Yeah," she said. "I'm trying to track down your little old crazy guy but so far, no luck."

"It's ok," Pat said. "I found him."

"What do you mean you found him?" she asked, again upset that the effort she had been putting forward was unnecessary.

"I went by and saw Bill Hammonds again this morning," Patrick said. "He offered up the information pretty quickly once he, um," Patrick paused, not wanting to alarm his sister. "Once he saw how I look."

"How do you look?" she asked.

"I had an interesting night last night. Can I treat you to dinner? I'll tell you all about it."

"Sure," she said. "I can meet you somewhere in an hour. Where do you want to go?"

"It seems like Applebee's is the only non-fast food joint around. How about there?"

"Ok, see you soon."

Elizabeth finished up the few details she needed to take care of during her planning hour then drove to Applebee's. When she got there she noticed Patrick's truck sitting in the parking lot. She pulled in beside him.

"Oh my God," she said, her right hand covering her open mouth. "What happened to you?"

Her brother had a black eye, a nasty welt across his left cheek, and his right hand was in a cast.

"I had a run in with some firewood last night," he said. "I was cutting wood really late and got caught in the dark and the rain. I was dumb enough to try carrying an armful of wood down the hill to the cabin in the dark when, 'whoop!'" Patrick threw his arms in the air and leaned back, simulating falling. "My feet went out from underneath me and I ran into a tree. The fire wood crushed my hand and punched me in the face."

"So how bad is the damage?" Elizabeth asked, a look of agony on her face.

"I broke two bones in my hand, just behind my middle and ring finger." He was indicating the bones on his good hand with the index finger of his bandaged hand.

"Let's get a table," he said. "I'm hungry. I was waiting to see a doctor most of the day."

Inside Elizabeth ordered a grilled, oriental chicken salad. Patrick got his Applebee's usual; the cowboy burger. A big, ground beef patty covered with barbeque sauce and onion straws.

"So why was it so important for you to find this old crazy guy you say you've found?" Elizabeth asked.

"There have been a lot of strange things that happened on that mountain that cannot be explained." Patrick said, slurping sprite through a straw. "Murders, disappearances, suicides. All kinds of things."

"So what does a crazy guy a thousand years old have to do with any of that?" she asked, slurping diet coke.

"I read an article in the old News Leader from more than half a century ago," Patrick said, looking around, making sure no one was listening. "He was supposedly hearing voices and seeing things. Something about Indian battles or something."

"You still haven't answered my question," Elizabeth said. "What does that have to do with anything?"

"I think he might know why the things that happen on that mountain happen," Patrick said.

"Have YOU seen anything happen on that mountain?" she asked. She felt that he must have to have such an interest in land deeds and a crazy old man.

"Like I'm gonna fall for that," he said, sitting back in his booth."

"What's that supposed to mean?"

"You're one degree below a shrink," he said. "I tell you anything that I've seen, or think I might have seen, and you blast me with a label. I bet you have a friend you can send me to who can put me on some kind of pills."

"Only if you need them Pat," she said. "I'm joking!" she quickly followed up when she saw that he wasn't laughing. "Level with me. Why all this interest?"

Patrick leaned over the table, looking around again, as if getting ready to tell a secret.

He was.

"Can I trust you?" he said, still looking around.

"Of course you can," she said. "I'm your sister."

"Fork Mountain is haunted!" he said, just as the waitress brought their food.

Elizabeth was anxious to get an explanation. She had to wait thirty seconds or so while she went through the expected pleasantries with the waitress who had just delivered their food. Yes, the food looked good. No, they didn't need anything else.

"What do you mean Fork Mountain is haunted?" Elizabeth finally spoke once the waitress had left. She said it, leaning forward, as if to whisper herself, but she hadn't whispered. It was more of a "your crazy," way of saying it.

"I've been seeing things up there, Elizabeth," he said, sinking his teeth into his burger, sauce running down the pinky of his left hand, and into the bandages covering the pinky on his right. Having his hand in a cast was something he was going to have to get used to. At least for a while. He quickly grabbed his napkin and started wiping the sauce off before it could leak all the way into the cast.

"What have you seen?" she asked, still leaning over the table, as if her food she had been looking forward to so much had not yet arrived.

"I've been seeing ghosts of course," he said. "Three little girls, a beautiful young woman and a mean old man."

"Three little girls, a beautiful young woman and a mean old man?" she said. "What the heck are you talking about?"

"You'd better eat before your chicken gets cold," he said, an attempt to get her off of the table. She was looking quite ridiculous now. She had been leaning forward further and further each time she repeated everything he had told her in the form of a question. She was now practically lying on the table, her hair now falling into her salad. Fortunately the dressing had been put on the side.

"Give me some details, Pat," she said, now forking salad into her mouth, looking around to make sure no one had witnessed her behavior.

Patrick gave her all of the details while they ate. He told of Sarah showing up that very first morning selling girl scout cookies. He told of Trixie and her thieving little ways. He mentioned their friend Amelia. He talked about meeting Amy at the swimming hole.

"It all clicked when I went to the library and found the news articles," he continued. He told Elizabeth every detail of all the articles. He even told her of the one regarding Grady Haines and why it was so important to find him.

"Sooo," she said, drawing it out, being skeptical. "What about the old man ghost? You didn't mention anything about him."

"Yeah," Patrick said nervously, placing his half eaten burger on his plate. "There's something about him that I haven't told you."

"You haven't told me anything about him, Pat."

Leaning over the table, just as his sister had done earlier, he whispered, "He did this to me."

"Did what to you?"

"He beat the crap out of me!"

"You got your butt kicked by the ghost of an old man?" Elizabeth said incredulously, just as the waitress showed up to check on their table.

"Do you… need anything else?" the teenaged girl asked nervously.

"No," Elizabeth waved her away, ignoring the fact that she was being rude.

"What do you mean an old man ghost beat the crap out of you?"

"He was chasing after the girls," he said. "They were so scared. I wasn't going to let him hurt them."

"He was chasing the girls?" she asked, one eyebrow raised. "By that you mean, the girl ghosts?"

"Yes," he said "I had to stop him."

"Sooo," she drew the word out again. "What happened next?"

"I chased him into the house. The girls had gone there and he went after them. I went in to stop him from hurting them and we got into a fight. As you can see," he said, voice now slower than the frantic rant it had just been in, "I got the short end of the stick."

"Patrick? She asked, now that she could tell he was done with his story.

"Yes?" he said.

"Do you want my professional, only one degree from a shrink opinion?"

"Yes," he said, now leaning over the table again.

"You're crazy! I'd stick with the firewood story."

After finishing dinner with Elizabeth, Patrick headed for Richwood. He had hoped that Elizabeth would at least be open to the events that were taking place on Fork Mountain. He wanted her in his corner. He had even hoped that she would go with him to visit Grady Haines. However, it was obvious that she didn't believe a thing he had told her.

Bill Hammonds had not given any more information about Haines the first time Patrick had met with him other than a simple mention of the man and his alleged mental condition. Patrick wasn't so sure that the man was crazy. He himself had now seen too many things on the mountain to discount anything he had not seen.

When he had gone back to Bill's house this morning before going to the doctor in Summersville, Patrick pleaded for information on Haines. He didn't have to tell Bill why he needed to know and Bill hadn't asked. Patrick had reason to believe that Bill might have known a little more about Fork Mountain than he had led on to know. It now made sense to Patrick why Bill had tried changing the subject when the graves came up the first time they had met.

Bill Hammonds informed Patrick that in the 1980's, while most of the "nuts were being put out on the street," as Elizabeth had referred to it, the serious cases were moved to assisted living. Grady Haines had been transferred to an assisted living facility in Lewisburg, West Virginia and had been there ever sense. Patrick called the institution on his cell phone on his way to Summersville and was happy to see that he indeed was still there.

Now though, he had the problem of driving there and visiting with Mr. Haines alone.

HEATHER!

Why had he not thought of it before? It would give the two of them, or three of them if she chose to take Caleb, more time together. Heather might actually be agreeable to the idea since her son was now seeing one of the same ghosts that he was.

"Heather?" he said when she answered the phone. He had started calling her number as soon as the idea of taking her with him entered his mind.

"Hi, Pat," she said, excited. He was glad she was happy to hear from him.

"Would you like to take a road trip later this week?" he said.

"Sure," she said. "I have tomorrow off."

"Don't you want to know where we are going?" Patrick said, laughing.

"Oh," she said. "Uh, well, yeah. Where are we going?"

"Lewisburg," he said. "To visit a patient at the Lewisburg Assisted Living Community."

"Why," she asked, now interested in the point of the trip. "Do you have a relative there?"

"No," he said. "Has Caleb said anything about seeing Sarah lately?"

"Yes," she said. "As a matter of fact, he said that she wants to know when we are coming back up to see you. He said she wants to play with him again. What is going on Pat? Is this related to your and my son's imaginary friend?"

"Kinda," Patrick said. "Look, I'm on my way from Summersville. Can I stop by and explain things to you when I get into town?"

"Sure," she said. "Caleb and I have already eaten. He'll entertain himself while we talk. I don't want him to hear. I am really concerned about what has been going on."

"Oh, you'll be even more concerned once you see me," he said.

"Why?" she asked. "Are you ok?"

"Oh yes," he said. "I'll be fine. I'll explain when I get there. I'll see you in about half an hour."

"Ok," she said, before hanging up the phone, puzzled.

#

"Oh my God!" Heather said when she opened the door. "What happened?"

"It's part of what I have to tell you," he said. "I should have come here first. I just had dinner with Elizabeth at Applebee's. She said she wouldn't repeat anything I had told her to my mom but I'm sure they're on the phone right now writing me off as crazy."

"Come in," she said, holding the door for him. "Caleb, Pat is here," she said as they made their way through the living room. Caleb was sitting on the couch, Lelo and Stitch on the television.

"Hi, Pat," the boy said, not looking in his direction.

"Hello, Caleb," Patrick said, noticing how the boy was looking in the direction of the television. He had never spent any time at all around blind people and was amazed at how similarly a blind child watched television to a child that could see.

"Oh yes," Heather said when she noticed him looking. "Blind kids watch T.V. too. Who knows how the characters look in his mind though?"

Patrick and Heather made their way into the kitchen and sat at the table.

"So what happened?" she asked, wanting to get straight to the story, not even offering him anything to drink.

"I'll start at the beginning," Patrick said. He then told the same story to Heather that he had told to Elizabeth. He included every detail down to the news paper articles and the storm that seemed to come and go with the old man's ghost. He even mentioned the strange, blue craw fish that seemed to come and go with the old man himself. He had started referring to them as "ghost crabs."

"So why can Caleb see Sarah?" was Heather's first question when he had finished.

"Sarah told me I could see her because I was 'broken,'" he said. "I think it is because I am emotionally broken because of what happened to Samantha."

"So you are telling me that my son is broken?" she asked, defensively.

"No," he said. "He seems to be so happy. Maybe he can sense her though because he is blind?"

Heather sat back in her chair, thinking. She was silent for a few seconds.

"They say that if you lose one sense, your other senses become heightened," Patrick offered.

"So how will going to Lewisburg to talk to some old crazy guy in an assisted living facility help anything?" she finally spoke.

"I don't think he is crazy," Patrick said. "I think that for some reason, the spirits on the hill decided to reveal themselves to him as well. Perhaps they showed him too much and he freaked out? Maybe he didn't freak out at all? Perhaps people just didn't believe him and wrote him off as crazy? It is worth a try though. I feel like there is something I can do. Like the girls are coming to me for help."

"I'll go with you Pat," she said. "I'm not saying I believe all of this, I'm saying I'll go with you. If nothing turns up, will you promise me that you'll talk to someone?"

"Heather," he said. "I know I sound crazy, but I've really been seeing the things I've told you about. Look at me!" he said, sitting back in his chair now as well.

"Like I said, I'll go with you. We can leave as soon as I drop Caleb off at school. We should have time to get there, talk to him and make it back by the end of the school day."

"That's all I'm asking for Heather. That's all I'm asking for."

#

Patrick resisted the urge to stop by his mother's house when he drove by after leaving Heather's. He would love to see her, even just to say hello, but he knew that his current condition would indeed send her over board. It was hard to tell what she might be thinking as well now that Elizabeth had no doubt called her the minute she had left the restaurant.

He kept driving, heading toward the top of Fork Mountain. He caught himself looking into the sky, making sure there were no rain clouds. He knew it didn't matter that the sky was now clear. It seemed the sky had been perfectly clear both times that the ghost of the old man had shown himself. Patrick hoped that he would not decide to do so tonight. One beating was enough in one twenty four hour period.

He reached his cabin, parked, then went inside. It was almost dark. He lit one of the oil lamps in the living room, grabbed three cold beers and his folding chair and headed out to the porch. He hoped that a couple deer or a bear would be all that he would see this evening.

"Working on your twelve ounce curls I see?" the voice came from the edge of the field. Amy was making her way over to him.

"Ah great," he mumbled under his breath.

"Is it a bad time?" she asked. She had heard him. But how? He had barely heard himself.

"No, Amy," he said, apologetically. "You are always welcome here any time you want to come.? He noticed that she was still wearing her short shorts. Thinking on it, he realized these were the same shorts she had been swimming in when they had first met. She had worn a bikini top that day. Perhaps it was under the plain, white tee shirt that she now wore, the same one she had on the other day.

"So I'd ask why you drink so much again but you'd probably just ask me why I walk so much, huh?" she said, now sitting down cross legged in the grass in front of him, just as she had the last time she visited.

"Amy," he said. "I know about you. I know who you are."

"What do you mean, you know who I am?"

"I have been doing some research," he told her. "I know who all of you are. I know about the little girls. I know they went missing." He paused respectfully before speaking again. "I know that you drown while swimming at the falls."

"I drown?" she asked.

"Yes," he said. "I can actually remember when it happened. You were several years older than me. I was in grade school at the time. I never knew you because of our age difference."

"So I drown," she said, trailing off. "Well, obviously, you don't know as much as you think you know."

"What do you mean?" he asked, thinking that perhaps she thought she was still alive.

"You say you know about the little girls," she said, taking the focus of the conversation off of herself. "Do you know about the old man?"

"No," he said. "I mean, I've had a run in with him, hence the black eye and broken hand. What do I need to know about him? Who is he?"

"Sounds to me like there's more you need to learn," she said, standing up and brushing off her shorts.

"Why don't you tell me about him?" he said.

"I have learned that it is best not to speak his name or of him," she said, looking around nervously. "He can tell. Let's talk about something else."

"Ok," he said. "Anything you want to talk about."

Looking at ease, she sat back down.

"Have you seen Phillip yet?" she asked, smiling.

"A few times," he said. "He's your father isn't he?"

"Yes," she said. "I have tried to communicate with him so many times, but he refuses to see me."

"Why is that, Amy? He can see the others. He has told me he has."

"I think it is because he refuses to accept that I'm gone," she said, a thoughtful look on her face. "He just won't let me go."

"Do you want him to let you go?"

"Not completely," she said. "You never can all the way you know?"

"Yeah," Patrick said, looking down, saddened. "I know."

"So what is your story?" she asked. "There has to be a reason you can see us. Come on. Who am I going to tell? I'm a ghost." She laughed as she said this, letting Patrick know that she was fully aware of the fact that she was dead.

Patrick opened up and told Amy everything about Samantha. He talked with her about the guilt he had for leaving her for a year to chase the all mighty dollar in Iraq as a civilian contractor.

"I don't know what I was thinking?" he said. "I didn't have a kid just to run off and leave her to fend for herself in this nasty world!"

He opened another beer. It was his third. He had drunk the other two while talking to Amy.

"So now I know why you drink so much," she said, voice low, eyes toward the ground. "It isn't helping you know. I'm sure that your daughter wouldn't want you to be treating yourself this way. As a matter of fact I know she wouldn't. I worry about my dad so much."

"Hey!" Patrick said. "Is there a way you guys can arrange for me to see Samantha?" His eyes lit up. There was excitement in his voice for the first time in a long time.

"I'm sorry Pat," Amy said. "I'm a ghost, not God. If there were, and I knew how, I would. I really wish I could."

"Yeah," he said, voice trailing off, his excitement now gone. "I appreciate it Amy."

"You listen closely to whatever the man you are going to see tells you tomorrow," she said, now rising.

"I didn't tell you anything about that," he said, curious. "How did you know?"

"I can sense things," she said. "I can read some of your thoughts. That's how I know a little more about you than you think. I knew you weren't killing yourself with alcohol for no reason, but I could also sense that you were blocking the thoughts that drove you to drink. You didn't strike me as a social drinker," she said, motioning all around the area with her hands.

"Yeah," he said. "Unless you count the wild life as bar mates."

"I have to go now Pat," she said. "I'll be back. Just remember what I said. Listen carefully tomorrow."

Patrick watched as Amy walked away. Again, like last time, she was not walking toward the graves, but toward the road to head off the hill. He watched her go, until in an instant, she was gone. She had not gone around the bend, or behind the trees. She had been there, in the open. Then all of a sudden, she simply vanished.

"He has been Meriwether Lewis for about a week now," the nurse, Brenda said in a hushed tone as she led Patrick and Heather up a final flight of steps. "He was George Washington last time."

"How often does he change characters?" Patrick asked. Heather listened intently.

"Usually weekly," Brenda said, now staring through the glass pane used to see into Grady Haines' room. "For some reason he has been stuck on Meriwether Lewis a little longer than usual."

"Does he ever become violent?" Heather asked, fearing what might be in store for her and Patrick this afternoon.

"Only once," Brenda said, turning to face her. "Unfortunately he was Adolph Hitler for a few days and he was convinced I was Jewish."

"Oh my God!" Patrick said with a laugh. "I don't mean to laugh, I'm sure that was uneasy for you."

\#

Grady Haines paced the floor in front of the large, center window overlooking the courtyard. The town's people below and just outside the gate went about their daily affairs without a care in the world.

"Captain Clark will come for me, Captain Clark will come for me," he said to himself over and over, wringing nervous, trembling hands.

A knock came at the door and he hustled to hide behind the large Victorian sofa at the end of the long room.

"Who goes there?" he said, terrified.

"It is me Captain Lewis," came Brenda's friendly voice. "I brought you lunch. I have a couple of guests who have traveled far to meet you."

"Have they brought Captain Clark?" he asked in a hopeful tone, certain his friend had come to save him.

"They have not," Brenda regretfully informed them. "But they speak highly of him as they do you. They have waited oh so long to meet you," she finished, ushering her two guests into the large forth floor room. This was the top floor of the assisted living facility located in the small, Appalachian town of Lewisburg, West Virginia. The town sat on the border with neighboring Virginia. With less hills and more fields than the rest of West Virginia, Patrick had always thought it should have been left behind in Virginia when the states separated in 1863.

"What has the slave woman prepared for lunch today?" the labeled lunatic asked as he made his way to the dining table set up in the middle of his room where Brenda placed a covered dish.

"Cornish hen," she replied, lifting the plastic lid to reveal a glob of geletal meat, overcooked macaroni and cheese and a gooey brown substance that barely passed health department standards as brown beans. Grady acted as if he saw a full bird, steaming, presented on a silver platter.

Taking up the plastic fork provided with the meal, he took a large portion of the brown goo into his mouth, savoring it before swallowing.

"Tell the slave girl she has done an exceptional job. Give her extra meat from the pig that she is to prepare for tonight's dinner. There is no need for her to live on chitterlings alone," he said as he took the cup of water laced with his dissolved medications. He held it, but did not drink it. He placed it back on the table and continued eating.

"As you wish, Captain Lewis," Brenda said, sneaking a grin toward her two guests.

"These fine folks are Patrick and Heather," Brenda said, introducing Grady's guests to him. "They've come to talk to you a little bit today."

"Oh, you must be the biographer from the University of Pennsylvania?" the old man said, eyebrows raised.

Brenda looked at Pat. The look on her face was saying, 'go along with it.'

"Uh, yes," Patrick said. "We are here to ask you some questions about your life."

"Yes," Grady said. "The great college founded by Dr. Franklin. Were you fortunate enough to meet Dr. Franklin before his passing?"

"We were not Sir," Patrick said. "But we have made several acquaintances among those who knew him and they speak highly of him."

"As they should," Grady spoke with a full mouth. "He was so instrumental in forming this great land of ours. If only he could have lived long enough for me to have reported to him in person all of the findings we made on our great journey."

"I'll leave you to talk with your guests now if that is alright with you, Captain Lewis," Brenda said, moving about the room, tidying up after him.

"As you wish," he said. He then faced his guests. "You no doubt want to hear of our run-ins with the natives across the great plains and west of the Rockies?"

"For certain, Captain Lewis," Heather said. "I admire a man of your bravery and knowledge and thirst to gain as much of it as I can for myself." She too was now in role playing mode.

"I hope that Brenda makes your stay as comfortable as possible," Grady said, turning to direct his comments toward Brenda.

"I will see to just that Captain Lewis," Brenda assured him, finishing up the tight corners on the hospital bed. She was sure that he saw a large, king sized bed with a goose down mattress as opposed to the twin size bed with the standard, institutional foam pad on top of the uncomfortable metal frame.

"I will leave you alone now Captain," Brenda said, shaking her head toward Patrick and Heather, assuring them they would be safe.

"I bid you good morrow," he spoke, shoveling the beans into his mouth, appearing to savor their flavor.

#

"This stuff is terrible!" Grady said, spitting the beans out of his mouth after Brenda shut the door. "I can't believe I've managed to stay alive all these years on what they feed me!"

Patrick and Heather looked at each other, puzzled. Grady had gone from loving his meal, as if it were the finest ever prepared, to spitting it out on his plate. Where they witnessing him changing characters?

"What the heck happened to you?" Grady asked. "Looks like you got the tar beat out of ya."

"I did, Captain," Patrick said.

"Ah, you can cut out that Lewis and Clark crap now that she's gone," Grady said, head motioning toward the door Brenda had exited. "My name's Grady Haines and I don't for a minute think I'm Meriwether Lewis, George Washington, Jesus Christ or anyone else. Shoot, I was only Hitler there for a few days because that winch pissed me off."

The old man rose out of his chair, taking up his cup of water. He walked over to a small sink in his room, dumped the water out then rinsed and refilled the cup.

"They've been putting my meds in my water for years. I aint drinking that stuff!" He took a big drink of the water, nearly emptying the cup. He turned around, filled it once again to the top, then returned to his seat.

"Well ain't you two gonna sit?" he said, looking at Patrick and Heather. Their mouths were gaping open. They couldn't believe what they were seeing. They had come here thinking the man might be crazy. His little Meriwether Lewis skit had convinced them that he was. Now they didn't know what to think.

They reluctantly pulled out the chairs on the side of the table opposite Grady. They sat down, never taking their eyes off of him, still silent, knowing not what to say.

"Don't worry," he said. "I aint gonna hurt ya. Do you know how long its been since I've talked to someone else who wasn't crazy?"

"So that was all an act?" Heather asked.

"Has been for nearly sixty years now," Grady said, shoveling macaroni and cheese in his mouth. He had the weekly meals memorized. The macaroni and cheese was the most edible part of this one so he always ate it, hoping it would come close to filling him so he wouldn't have to eat most of the rest. "Once you get stuck with a label, you're just that. Stuck! The treatments may have gotten more humane through the years, but this sugar coatin' political correctness crap sure has made it hard to shed the labels."

"So you're not crazy?" Patrick said.

"So I take it you're the smart one," Grady said to Heather, a sly look then given to Patrick.

"How do you know so much about the characters you portray?" Patrick asked, ignoring the non-verbal insult.

"It's called reading," the old man said, now shoveling more macaroni and cheese in his mouth. "I doubt kids your age do much of it."

Patrick and Heather glanced around and saw that other than the sparse furniture in the room, there were books everywhere. They filled the few books shelves that were in the room and were piled three feet deep on the floor.

"They limit my television time to one hour a day so I read most of the time," Grady continued. "Not that there's anything on there to watch anyway. Never was. What do you two want anyway? You look a little old to be students workin' on a term paper."

"We've come to ask you about Fork Mountain," Patrick said, getting right to the point of their visit.

Grady stopped chewing. He placed the plastic fork on the tray and looked Patrick square in the eye. He was motionless for a minute. He swallowed the macaroni that was in his mouth.

"No one's asked me about that place in years," he said. "What do you want to know about it?"

"We've heard you saw things up there that drove you," Patrick paused… "crazy."

"Them things I said I seen, I seen!" Grady said forcefully. "It didn't drive me crazy. People just didn't want to believe it! They were gonna let me out back in the 1980's when they let the real crazies out. I didn't have nowhere else to go except back to that mountain so I became a right good actor," he said with a wink toward Heather.

"I've been seeing things up there too," Patrick said. "I believe you."

"What have you seen?" Grady asked.

Patrick explained everything he had witnessed on the mountain, just as he had to Elizabeth and Heather the evening before. Grady listened intently, forgetting about his barely edible meal.

"I never seen any of that," Grady said. "Makes sense though. All that would have happened after I left." Grady picked up his fork. He didn't eat. He swirled the fork around in the goo on his tray, thinking about what Patrick had just told him.

"Makes a lot of sense about the kids too," the old man spoke again. "Especially the little girls."

"What do you mean?" Heather asked. "What did you see?"

"What I saw was shown to me on three separate occasions," Grady said, putting down the fork and leaning back in his chair. "I never really understood what exactly it was that I was witnessing until about twenty years ago. I ran across a book the local high school had donated here and it all made sense. Or at least it made more sense. At least what I saw did."

"What was it you saw?" Patrick asked, his curiosity killing him. "What book?"

Grady rose from his chair and went to one of the book shelves. "I keep the good ones up here," he said, his index finger in search of the title. "Here it is," he said, pulling a solid black book with white lettering off of the shelf. He walked back over and placed it on the table in front of Patrick.

"You can have this," he said. "I'm ninety three years old. I don't think I'll have time to read it again."

The book was titled, "History of the Early Settlement and Indian Wars of West Virginia." It had been written by Wills De Hass in 1851.

"It had originally been titled, 'History of the Early Settlement and Indian Wars of Western Virginia,'" Grady said. "They changed the title in later printings after the states split. Everything in the book took place in what is now West Virginia. It lists the accounts of the settlers going back prior to the Revolutionary War through about 1795."

"What does this book have to do with what is going on on top of Fork Mountain?" Patrick asked.

"There ya go," the old man said, sitting back into his chair, making himself comfortable. "Tryin' to get outta reading aint ya?"

"We really need your help," Heather pleaded. "My son might be part of what is going on here."

"I'll tell you what I saw," the old man said. "You'll have to take what I tell you, take what you've seen, read the book and piece it all together."

"I'll only tell you on one condition though," Grady said, just as Patrick and Heather thought he was about to start his tale.

"Anything," Patrick said.

"Don't mention a word to Brenda or anyone else about me not being crazy," Grady said. "If you do, they might let me out of here. I would rather die here of old age than go back to that mountain and die only God knows how."

"I believe it was the fall of 1952, the first time I saw something up there," Grady said, leaning back in his chair, his hands joined together at the fingertips. "I used to hunt on top of that mountain all the time. I could go twenty minutes from the house and take my pick of turkeys, deer or squirrels."

"We used to actually own that land when I was a boy," he said, thoughtfully. "Momma got herself in, how shall I say it, a 'bind' and had to get rid of it. That crooked Judge Gilbert ended up getting it."

Grady thought it would be a good time to change the subject. He didn't know how much Patrick and Heather knew, if anything, of his own family's past. He didn't want to fill them in more if they knew anything or enlighten them if they knew nothing.

"The Smith family bought it from the judge and they later sold it to the Ables brothers. I think they might'a broke even on the deal, the Smith's."

Though Patrick knew of this history, he kept his poker face on. He didn't reveal to Grady through words or body language that he had any clue.

"I was up there that fall," Grady continued. "I was in the area there were those graves are. I'd seen a huge buck up there the time before that and I was waitin' there to see if he'd come back."

"Well, I was sittin' up against this big oak tree when I heard twigs crackling and branches on the ground snappin'. I knew something was coming my way. But when I looked over expectin' a deer, why I saw these two little Indian girls."

"Indian girls?" Heather asked. "Have you seen any Indian girls?" she asked Patrick.

"No," he said. "All the girls I have seen have been white."

"Are ya gonna let me tell it or ain't ya?" Grady said, none too happy that he had been interrupted.

"I'm sorry," Heather said, a look on her face as if she had been disciplined by her teacher in school.

"Alright then," Grady said. "So I see these two little Indian girls. I tried to speak to them and they didn't even hear me. At least they didn't let on like they heard me. They just kept on lookin' at the ground while they walked."

"Anyway," he continued. "I just watched 'em, rubbin' my eyes to make sure I was really seein' 'em. Why, they was probably eight and ten years old or so. Pretty as could be. Long black hair pulled back into two pig tails goin' down the sides of their heads."

"Looked like they were gathering acorns. They were pickin' 'em up and puttin' 'em in these little baskets they had that looked like they were made out of deer hide. They must have been there alone like that for ten minutes or so, then this Indian woman came out. I was thinking' it must have been their mother. They sure did favor her. Looked just like her."

Patrick and Heather were going back and forth between exchanging blank looks at each other, and staring in awe at Grady Haines while he told his story. They were hanging on every word.

"Well, the little girls went skipin' off through the woods with their mother," Grady continued. "When they got outta site I got up and went after 'em. I didn't see 'em any more once they crossed over the knoll there where the graves are. I looked everywhere and it was like they had vanished."

"I went home and told my sister what I'd seen," he said, coming out of his trance like state, exchanging looks from Patrick to Heather. "I wasn't married and neither was she. She was stayin' with me at the time. That was common back then ya know?"

Patrick and Heather shook their heads up and down, letting the man know they were following. Patrick was now remembering the story of Grady's family history that Bill Hammonds had relayed to him. He had not shared the story with Heather. He wanted her to be as unbiased as she could be in regard to Grady's mental state.

"She just got angry with me and told me I was always comin' up with the wildest tales," Grady said. "I told her it weren't no tale. I told her I saw it with my own eyes, but she just told me she didn't want to hear no more about it."

"So I never saw them little girls again, till that one time," Grady said, voice trailing off. "Oh I wish I hadn't seen that, what they went through."

"What did you see?" Heather asked. "What happened to them?"

"Well," Grady said. "I have to tell it in order, see. Let me tell ya about what I saw that next spring."

"Ok," Patrick said. He was paying very close attention, trying to figure it out.

"So the next spring I was up there a spring gobbler huntin'," Grady said. "There were so many gobblers on that hill ya didn't have to worry about over sleepin' in the springtime. Why they'd start goin' off as soon as the sun was comin' up. You could hear 'em all the way down at the house. Why, when I'd hear 'em in the spring, I'd just grab my old twenty gauge and head up there to see if I could take one of their heads off."

"So I'm up there, sitting in the same place, close to the graves. As so often times happened, the minute I get up there them darn birds go quiet, and there I am tryin' to call 'em up."

"I give a couple calls then I start hearin' some bangin' around down in the field below the graves. I go over to the edge of the hill there and look down, and I swear I see folks, white folks, dressed the way the early settlers of that area might have dressed. They were wearing overalls, wide brimmed hats and boots made outta treated leather."

"How many did you see?" Patrick asked.

"Just three at first," Grady said. "There were two men and what looked like a teenage boy. They were workin' the field. Looked like they were getting' ready to plant."

"Did you try speaking to them?" Heather asked.

"No," Grady said. "I figured if those little Indian girls didn't' hear me, or just didn't want to talk that these folks wouldn't either. You know, that house down there that the Smith's had, this was during the time they owned the land, was already there. I knew the family used it more as a get away than a home. No one lived there all the time. I couldn't figure out why there'd be people down there diggin' up the field. Especially dressed the way they were."

"You said there were just three at first," Heather added. "Did more people show up?"

"Oh yeah," Grady said. "I sat down on the hill there and watched for a while. Eventually a woman and a teenage girl came out. They had food. They came out to feed the men folk."

"So then what?" Patrick asked. He felt like a kid again, sitting around the campfire listening to ghost stories.

"Well, after they ate, it looked like they all went inside, but I knew the Smith's kept that place locked up," Grady said. "After they were in, I walked down off the hill. I had to go through a pretty thick patch of woods that was in between me and them. Why, when I came out of it, everything looked different. The ground hadn't been broken at all. There weren't no farmin' equipment nowhere."

Patrick and Heather gave each other a wide eyed look.

"I went over to the house," Grady said, "And the door was locked. From the outside! It had a big padlock on it. I was sure I saw them go in the house."

"So then what?" Heather asked.

"So then I went back home and told my sister what I had seen. Just like the time before, with the Indian girls, she told me that I had to stop goin' in the woods and comin' out with these tall tales. I told her it weren't no tale, that I had seen what I seen, but she didn't believe me. She got madder than the last time I told her about what I seen."

"You said what you saw happened on three different occasions," Pat said, leaning forward, even more intently than he had been before. "What happened on that third occasion?"

"Ah, it was awful," Grady said. "Just awful. I hate to even think about it."

"We have to know!" Heather said.

"Ok," Grady said. "I'll tell it. It might be hard though, reliving what I saw. It was the most awful thing I could imagine people doin' to each other. I guess it happened a lot back then though."

Patrick and Heather were speechless. They simply listened, remaining silent. They were allowing the old timer to get in the proper mode to tell the final installment of his tale.

"It was the summer of '53," the old man finally spoke, having settled back into his chair, getting comfortable. "I was just up there a walkin' one evening. Just before dark. I made my way up to those old graves."

"Just as I got there, here come those two little Indian girls again. Why, they was so cute. They had on these little skirts made outta deer hide. They had their baskets with them and they were pickin' flowers."

"Even though they hadn't spoke to me the only other time I saw them, I tried taklin' to 'em again. They never spoke this time either. It was like they couldn't see me."

"So, I just sat down there and watched 'em play. They'd take turns puttin' flowers in each other's hair. Then their momma came out, just like last time. Boy was she a looker! She had on a skirt too and I tell ya, her legs! Why, I ain't never seen legs like that on a white woman."

Heather blushed. Patrick smiled.

"Well, the mother sat down there, just keepin' an eye on the girls. That's when I heard what sounded like something or someone sneakin' up behind me. I turned around and here come them two men that I'd seen down in the field the spring before. They was sneakin' up real tricky like."

"I saw the one man raise a rifle and aim it at the Indians. I stood up, right in between 'em! I put my hands up and yelled, 'NO!' It was too late though or he never heard me. He shot a round off. It seemed like it went right through me. It felt like a cold wind whispin' through my lungs." Grady shivered at the memory.

"Anyway, I turned around, and the Indian woman was layin' there dead. The two little girls were a shakin' her, like they were tryin' to wake her up from sleepin'. They was cryin' something awful."

"The two men didn't seem to care. They came up a runnin' and grabbed those little girls. They… they…"

"They what?" Patrick asked, his voice like a whisper.

"They took and bashed their heads into a tree," Grady said, tears running down his face.

"Oh my God," Heather gasped. She put a hand over her mouth and started crying too. Patrick noticed this. Any doubt he had as far as Heather believing the events that took place on top of Fork Mountain was now gone. He could tell she was believing every word Grady Haines spoke, as he was himself.

"That ain't the end of it though," Grady said, wiping away his tears.

"Just then, I seen this old Indian man, all made up in paint and make up, come riding on a horse at the top of the hill above the graves. He seen what the white men had done. Just then, half a dozen Indian men came running from out behind him. I never really saw them come from anywhere in particular. They just… appeared."

"The two white men heard 'em. They turned to shoot but it was too late. Those Indians were knockin' 'em over the head with tomahawks. Didn't kill 'em. Just knocked 'em out. Then they tied 'em up to the very tree they had bashed the girls heads in on."

"After they had 'em all tied up nice and tight, they went down off the hill. I stayed there, still as could be. I didn't know if they could see me or not, but I didn't want to take no chances. That old Indian was sittin' there on his horse. He never got off. He was just doing some kind of chant."

"Ten minutes later those Indian warriors came back up the hill. They had that teenaged boy, the teenaged girl and the white woman tied up. They were a kickin' and a screamin' but the Indians, why they'd just smack 'em around every time they let out a yell."

"They made all three of 'em get down on their knees in front of the two men they'd tied up to the tree. They'd woken up by now and knew what was going on."

"Those Indians killed those three people in front of the men. They didn't do it quick either. They bludgeoned them to death with their tomahawks. There was blood, must a been squirtin' out fifteen yards or more."

Heather turned away, as if she were going to be sick. Patrick was glad he had skipped breakfast or he might have been.

"After they killed the women and that boy, they did the same thing to the men," Grady said. "They stuck around and buried them. That's how those graves got there. They buried them where the graves are."

"After they were done, why those Indian warriors just vanished, like they were never there at all. They were though. I seen 'em. The old man in the paint though. He didn't just vanish. He did something first."

"What did he do?" Patrick asked.

"He cursed the land!" Grady said. "I believe that squaw was his daughter and them girls his grand daughters. He did some kind of Indian chant, then he spit on the ground. It was a curse. I know it was."

"That makes sense," Patrick said. "That is why all those little girls disappeared on Fork Mountain. The curse must have affected whoever it was that killed them. Made him live out the Indian's revenge all those years later."

"Wow," Heather said in disbelief, though she now believed all of it.

"If it was a curse, it was a strong one," Grady said. "It sounds like it has affected just about everyone who's spent too much time up there in some way."

Patrick took note of this statement. Had Samantha disappeared because of the amount of time he himself had spent on Fork Mountain? Could the curse have attached itself to him? Could it have stayed with him all those years then affected his daughter?

"Ok, Captain Lewis," Brenda said as she came into the room to take up Grady's tray. "Lunchtime and visiting hours are over."

"Did you compliment the slave girl?" Grady asked Brenda while she bent over to clear up his tray. He gave a secret wink to Patrick and Heather. They winked back.

"Oh yes," Brenda said. "She said for me to thank the masah."

"Well, I guess we should be off now," Patrick said, rising to his feet.

"Yes," Heather said, standing also. "We have to get to work on your biography. Philadelphia is a long ride from here."

"Now don't leave out the good parts," Grady said, sliding the book toward Patrick. He had almost forgotten it. He reached out and picked it up, placing it firmly against his chest.

"We won't forget, Captain," Patrick said. "We won't forget anything you've told us."

Patrick had taken the more scenic route of highways 39 and 219 to get to Lewisburg from Richwood. On the way back, he took interstate 64. His mind was too full, tossing around all the information Grady Haines had just given him, to pay attention to the scenery. It wasn't until they crossed the county line from Greenbrier back into Nicholas County that either of them spoke.

"That was some creepy stuff," Heather said, breaking the silence.

"So do you believe me now?"

"Yeah," she said. "I believe you."

More silence passed for several minutes before Patrick spoke again.

"I guess I'm just going to read the book and see what other piece of the puzzle it provides," he said, maneuvering the turns, now again on what would be considered back roads in most states, though they were the main means of travel in West Virginia. Narrow two lanes too often bogged down with timber and coal trucks.

"It sounds like the mystery may go back more than three hundred years," Heather said. "I'm curious to what might have happened up there over that time."

"I know," Patrick agreed. "We only know about a suicide, a murder that may also have been a suicide and some old man who is perfectly sane, yet has allowed himself to be locked up as a lunatic because he was too scared to go home. And all the missing girls."

"So what do you plan to do other than read the book?" Heather asked.

"I don't know yet," he said. "I feel like the girls want help. They seemed to appreciate it the other night when I got my butt kicked."

"That's probably the first time anyone has ever helped them," she said.

"Yeah," he said. "I still can't figure out what Amy was trying to tell me though."

"What do you mean?"

"I saw her again last night after I left your house," he said. "I was on the porch and she showed up to talk for a few minutes. She told me to pay very close attention to what Grady was going to tell me today. I did. I hung on his every word, but I don't know what she meant."

"The answer is probably right in front of your face," Heather said. "Maybe Amy knew that with the information Grady was going to give you, you'd be able to piece it all together."

"If so, I hope she was right," he said.

They made it back to Richwood with plenty of time for Heather to get Caleb from school. Patrick pulled up in front of her house to drop her off.

"Thanks for coming with me today, Heather," he said, looking at her after putting the truck in park.

She took the fingers of his bandaged hand into hers, the first time they had actually touched other than a friendly hug since his return to town. "You're welcome," she said, rubbing his fingers smoothly. "Any time I can be of help I will. I want to."

"Thanks," he said, smiling.

With that, Heather opened the door and got out. He watched to make sure she got into her house before pulling out. He had really enjoyed her company, not just because of the fact that he had someone to go with him, but because it was her.

Patrick made his way through the small town to head back up Fork Mountain, excited about reading the book Grady had given him. When he went past his mother's, he noticed that Elizabeth's car was parked out front. However, his mother's car was gone. Patrick assumed his mother and sister were out doing some bonding.

He continued up Fork Mountain, and upon reaching the point in the road where the trail got really rough, he saw his mother's car parked at the side of the road.

"Ah, great!" he said aloud. "Company."

He knew that his mother and sister had come up to see him. No doubt Elizabeth had told Ginny of his condition. He was certain she would have also told her about the story he had shared with her about the ghosts. A story that Elizabeth had refused to believe and that he was sure his mother would refuse to believe as well.

When he made it to his cabin on top of the mountain both women were sitting on the porch waiting on him. A few yards away Sarah, Amelia and Trixie were sitting in the grass staring at the two women. Patrick parked his truck and killed his ignition. How strange this image was. His mother and sister, and the ghosts of three little girls no more than a stone's throw away from them. He knew his mother and sister couldn't see the girls. How was he going to be able to ignore them in front of them?

"Hey guys," he said after closing the truck door. "Out for a little exercise?"

"Wow!" Ginny said. "Elizabeth told me you got pretty banged up. She wasn't lying. Are you ok?"

"Yeah, I'll be fine," he said. His hand was more sore now than it had been the night of the fight. His face felt better but he knew it didn't look better. As he walked up to his mother and sister on the porch, the three girls stood and walked behind him.

"Who are they?" Sarah asked.

"So, *Mom*," he said, placing emphasis on the word "mom" hoping that the girls would take the hint. "Did my LITTLE SISTER ELIZABETH here tell you what happened to me?" He emphasized these words again for the same reason.

"Oh," Amelia said.

"Yes, she did," Ginny said. "I got two different versions though. Which was it? You fell into a tree while carrying firewood or you got beat up by a ghost?"

"I fell into a tree carrying firewood," he said.

"Why are you lying, Pat?" Trixie asked. "Tell the truth."

"Sh," Patrick said.

"What?" Elizabeth asked.

"I was saying," Patrick stammered, "sh… should we go inside?"

"Sure," Ginny said. "I haven't been in here for years."

Patrick opened the door and led them in. The little girls followed Ginny and Elizabeth. Amelia pulled the door shut behind them.

"What was that?" Elizabeth asked, turning around, a bit startled.

"The wind must have picked up," he said, glaring at Amelia. "It is weird up here. It can be perfectly calm and then the wind or an odd storm blows in from nowhere."

"About the storms," Elizabeth said. "What was it you were saying about the storms appearing when the ghost of some old man shows up?"

"Don't talk about him!" Sarah yelled. Elizabeth heard nothing.

"I was pulling your leg, Elizabeth," Patrick said. "I figured why not have a little fun with you. It was a better story than just telling you that I ran into a tree. It's a little embarrassing really."

Trixie saw Samantha's cabbage patch doll sitting on the couch. She made her way to it and started to pick it up.

"Don't touch the doll!" Patrick said.

"What doll?" Ginny said, looking around.

"But you said I could play with it whenever I wanted as long as I came here to do it," Trixie said, giving him puppy dog eyes.

"Oh, was this Samantha's?" Ginny said, picking it up then sitting down on the couch.

"Yes," Patrick said. "I mean, don't take it. I like to keep it around."

Trixie glared at Ginny while she played with the doll. She was jealous.

"So," Ginny began. "I know you've been preoccupied with the disappearance of those little girls from so long ago. Elizabeth told me about that far fetched story you had told her. I knew you couldn't be serious but we thought we'd come up here and check on you."

"I appreciate it mom, but I'm fine. I think I have been spending a little too much time alone and I've been getting a little creative. Maybe I'll start writing or something."

"That would be good therapy, Pat," Elizabeth said, sitting down beside her mother. "We're just worried about you. I mean, you quit your high paying job in D.C. and came up on this mountain and started living like a hermit. It just seems strange."

"What's a hermit?" Sarah asked.

"A hermit," Patrick began. "A man who lives all alone in the woods and has nothing to do with other people."

"Oh," Sarah said. "We must be hermits," she directed toward the other two girls.

"But we're not men," Amelia said. "We're girls."

"Well," Ginny began. "You do live in the woods and spend most of your time alone."

"Not true," Patrick said. "Why, today I took Heather over to Lewisburg for lunch."

He was not lying entirely. He had taken Heather to Lewisburg, at lunch time. They hadn't actually eaten though.

"That's a good start," Elizabeth said.

Trixie pulled the doll off of Ginny's lap. Patrick rushed to take it from her immediately before she could run off with it.

"Hey!" she said, staring up at him. Her puppy dog eyes had now filled with anger.

"Sorry Pat," Ginny said. "I must have dropped it. It's like it just… fell off of my lap or something."

"It's ok," he said. "I just like to make sure that I take care of it. It was Samantha's favorite doll."

He came up with a plan.

"Give me just a minute," he said, then took the doll and headed for the stairs. He gestured with his head for the girls to follow him.

"Stay up here and be very quiet," he told the girls once upstairs. "I can't let them know that I can see you. Just play up here with the doll until they leave then you can come down stairs."

"I put it up there for safe keeping," he said of the doll when he got back down stairs.

"Look Pat," Elizabeth said. "I think you are depressed. I have a friend, a social worker for the county, who wouldn't mind talking to you a couple of times a week. It's only natural to be depressed after what happened. It might make you feel better."

"Yeah," Patrick agreed. "You know, I really have put off getting help and I'm almost ashamed of what I told you at the restaurant. I think I've been putting off dealing with reality for so long that I confuse myself with what is real and what isn't. I feel safer that way."

"That is some really good insight, son," Ginny said. "It's only natural. I got a little crazy in my head when your father passed away. Sure, he got on my nerves a lot and we got to spend over forty years together, but it is a major life change that doesn't come easy."

"You're right," he said. "Elizabeth, how about I give your friend a call in the next couple of days and see if I can set something up?"

"Would you really call him?" Elizabeth asked.

"Sure I will. I promise."

"Well, this went easier than I thought," Elizabeth said to her mother, smiling.

"Oh, was this an intervention?" Patrick asked.

"Yes," Elizabeth said. "I only wanted to do it because I care about you and I was worried. Especially after what you told me at the restaurant. All that horse sense about ghosts."

Upstairs, Trixie was jumping on the bed even though Sarah and Amelia had told her she'd better not.

"What was that?" Ginny asked, looking up toward the ceiling.

"What was what?" Patrick asked, acting as if he hadn't heard the banging noise.

"It sounded like a thump."

"Yeah," Elizabeth said. "I heard it too." Both of them looked at Patrick for an explanation.

"Oh," he said. "There are squirrels in the attic. Sometimes they are really loud," he said, rising to his feet, making his way to the steps heading upstairs. "You girls be quiet up there!"

"We told you so!" Amelia said to Trixie.

"What did you say?" Elizabeth asked, crinkling her face.

"I said, 'you squirrels be quiet up there.'"

"Oh," she said, shaking her head. "Sound doesn't travel well in this old cabin. I thought you said 'you girls be quiet up there.'"

"You sound crazy now, Sis," he said.

"Well, our work here is done," Ginny said, rising to her feet. "We'd better head off the mountain before it gets dark. Do you want to come eat with us?" she directed toward her son.

"No thanks," he said. "I picked up a book today in Lewisburg. I want to just take it easy this evening and do some reading."

"What book?" Elizabeth asked.

"Oh, just a book on West Virginia history," he said. "I get into that stuff sometimes. Want me to give you a ride down to your car?" He wanted to change the subject before any more questions could be asked.

"No thanks," Ginny said. "It is a beautiful day. It is so nice walking up here. I should come up more often."

"Yes you should," Patrick agreed. "Come up any time you want. It is good exercise and it is so serene up here in the woods. It has really been doing me a lot of good."

"Ok," Ginny said. "Come on Elizabeth. Let's go."

"Ok," Elizabeth said, rising to her feet.

"Pat," she said after opening the door. "I'll send you my friend's contact information in an email tomorrow. Make sure you call him ok?"

"I will," he said. He then followed them out the door and walked them to the edge of the field. "You guys be careful going down the mountain."

"Ok," his mother said, giving him a hug. Elizabeth gave him a hug as well. The women started walking down the road toward the car.

Patrick made his way back to the cabin. The girls had come down stairs and were waiting for him on the porch. Trixie was holding Samantha's doll in her arms, the look on her face saying, "don't you dare try to take this away from me."

"Why did you act like you couldn't see us?" Amelia asked. "Did we do something wrong?"

"No," Patrick said. "Not at all sweaty. You guys have never done anything wrong. It's just that, as you know, not everyone can see you. Those who can't see you don't believe those of us who can. They don't understand and they don't believe. I love having you guys around and didn't want to jeopardize our relationship. If my sister and mother thought… knew I was seeing you, they'd try to get me off of this mountain and make sure I never came back."

"We don't want you to leave," Sarah said. "You helped us the other night."

"I know," Patrick said. "That's why I acted like I couldn't see you. I want to help you as much as I can."

"If you leave, you have to let me keep the doll," Trixie said.

"I will," he said. "I love that doll, but I love you too. I love all of you guys. If I ever go anywhere I'll let you keep the doll."

"Promise you won't leave?" Sarah said.

Patrick thought back about another little girl who had said these exact words to him before he went to Iraq. He had not made this same promise to her, his daughter, and he had wanted to die most days since her disappearance because of it.

"I promise," he said. And he meant it.

18

The scene on the top of Fork Mountain for the rest of the evening was tranquil. Sarah, Amelia and Trixie played in the field; ring around the rosy, hide and seek, duck, duck goose. Trixie constantly had Samantha's doll with her, holding it as if it were an animate object itself. Patrick sat on the porch in his nylon folding chair, his face buried in the book Grady Haines had given him earlier in the day.

At one point he had gone into the cabin and brought out a cold beer. Popping the top then taking it to his lips, it was intercepted by the fair, beautiful hand of Amy.

"Drink this instead," she said, handing him a glass of water. He watched as she poured the beer on the ground. "You need to pay attention. You can't afford to get drunk and brush over any details." She spent the rest of the evening sitting in the field, exchanging glances from the girls to Patrick, making sure he was reading without drinking.

Though Patrick read the occasional novel, usually best sellers that he wanted to read in order to know what everyone was talking about, he rarely read books on history. This book, "The History of the Early Settlement and Indian Wars of West Virginia," was making him realize all that he had missed out on in the past. There were so many parts of the local history he was now learning about that he had never learned in school.

He was interested especially when he came to parts that discussed area's he had actually visited. He read of the Pringle brothers who had settled what is today known as Buckhannon, West Virginia. The brothers had gone out to hunt and stake claims to land and had actually spent two years living inside the hollowed out bottom of a giant sycamore tree. The book described it as being as large as an average sized cabin from back in those days. He knew the spot still existed as a tourist attraction in Upshur county and made a mental note to visit it someday.

Another historical fact he had never been aware of that drew particular interest was the concept of "tomahawk land laws." It seemed that back in the late 1600's, into the mid 1700's while this part of the new world was still being settled, all one had to do to lay claim to land was take an axe, or a tomahawk and cut a notch into a tree along a stream. The person then owned all the land extending from the stream for a considerable distance plus all the land along the stream until it flowed into another stream.

No wonder there was such a push for movement west. Who, in today's times, would not kill to have the opportunity to lay claim to land simply by putting a hatchet mark in a tree beside a stream?

This was all part of the establishment's plan at the time to settle the new world. The best way to spread the new Americans west was to offer them enough incentive, free land, to make the move. Sure, there were many new dangers such as Indians and ferocious animals that did not exist in the old world, like wolves and cougars but the desire to own land outweighed these threats in most people's minds and inspired them to move west. They did so, however, and unfortunately, destroying and killing many of these new things that they did not understand.

During those times, elk and mountain lions were as plentiful on the east coast as they are today on the west coast. However, they were often slaughtered in massive hunting parties called circle hunts.

Often, up to two hundred men or more would gather and form a radius up to a mile long, wide and deep. They would then push in toward each other, killing everything in their path. They would kill a dozen elk, dozens deer, numerous black bears, mountain lions, turkeys and squirrels. It was not uncommon for several men themselves to end up getting maimed or killed by a stray bullet or a wounded beast.

Patrick took an occasional break from reading to watch the girls play in the field. It was a beautiful, peaceful site. It was now turning to fall. The foliage was beginning to change. It was wonderful watching the three little girls enjoying themselves. He enjoyed watching Amy look on, looking quite beautiful as she did, with the reds, oranges, yellows and purples of the leaves in the background. There was still plenty of green but there wouldn't be for long. He found himself longing for Samantha to show up and join them, though he knew she wouldn't.

Though Patrick was enjoying his history lesson, he caught himself thinking, wondering actually, what any of it had to do with the unmarked graves and the story Grady Haines had told him. Then he got into the second half of the book which focused mostly on the Indian Wars.

Though merely a "spoke in the wheel" of the American, capitalistic society as much as any of his peers, he was smart enough to know that the powers that be, at any given time, had agendas. He saw enough of that when he was in Iraq. Frustrated soldiers, trained to fight, yet sent to Iraq where they were told they were not allowed to fire their weapon without facing serious backlash.

He knew farmers were paid, and had been for a generation now, NOT to grow certain crops so that the government could control the "supply versus demand" aspect of agriculture, thereby controlling the prices.

He knew too, that the Federal Reserve was perhaps the largest enslaver of human kind since the institution of slavery itself, controlling the world's economy with interest rates and money flow. Every dollar that was in circulation was loaned out at interest from the Federal Reserve, an organization run by world bankers who, unfortunately too many Americans actually believe was part of the federal government. It was nothing more than a private establishment hell bent on increasing the wealth of its members.

Patrick knew of the establishment's agenda in days gone by as well. Sure, most folks knew there was never anything to McCarthy's "red scare" but no one spoke out about it. Not even President Harry Truman at the time, who personally despised McCarthy. If the establishment could keep up the fear and paranoia toward communism and communists, they held a blank check to do anything they wanted in the name of fighting communism.

This led eventually to the war in Vietnam. A war in which US defense contractors actually made money by selling anti-aircraft weaponry to the North Vietnamese. Patrick could remember years later, when many of the ROE (rules of engagement) came out in Vietnam, and the uproar so many of the American people were in when it was found out that US pilots were NOT allowed to take out these defense systems until they were fully operational. If they had, the North Vietnamese would have stopped purchasing them, hence the US defense companies selling them would have stopped making money from both sides of the war. Patrick, and many other Americans wondered how many US planes were taken out by these systems once they were operational. One less plane might have meant a dead family member to several Americans back home, but it meant more money to the contractor by replacing the plane.

Patrick couldn't consider himself much above the people who didn't know of these agendas. He himself had been caught up in the most recent agenda. While many war opposing Americans back home were screaming about the war being for oil, Patrick knew differently. It was a war about infrastructure. Patrick had seen this with his own eyes while in Iraq.

He had avoided the misery of the life of an underpaid and overworked soldier. Instead, he took advantage of it as an overpaid, under worked civilian contractor. He had seen where the Iraqi's were receiving better plumbing systems than they had ever had. His line of work, however, was even more proof of the agenda.

What he learned, that most Americans were unaware of had to do with telecommunications. Iraq, being a very third world nation, had never benefited from the existence of land lines. However, with the advent of cell phone technology in the early 1990's their telecommunication methods took a giant leap into the twenty first century.

In the city of Mosul, for instance, there is more daily cell phone traffic among the population of roughly five million people than there is in New York and Los Angelas combined! This is due to the fact that cell phones are their only means of communication for the most part. The locals also used them for texting and their limited internet access.

At the beginning of the war, as is the case in most wars, the first target of the US armed forces was the country's communication systems. All telecommunication systems that were in place at the time were destroyed. Now, as companies like WorldCom and Sprint rebuild this infrastructure, they are also reaping the monetary benefits of the new system. With usage like that alone in Mosul, it was a new, huge market.

The folks back home, screaming about oil, could do nothing to make the military brass, top politicians in D.C. and the heads of these corporations happier. It was a fact that Patrick was aware of, that no major US oil company had been awarded any oil contracts by the new Iraqi government. They had all gone to European, Russian and Asian firms. However, if you watch what one neighbor is doing (oil) you won't see what the one on the other side of you is doing (infrastructure).

Based on this knowledge and awareness, Patrick could easily pick out the propaganda being disseminated at the time that the book he was now reading was published. That propaganda revolved around the Native American Indians. Stories were told in the book of terrible events such as Indians coming upon whites, bashing infant's heads into trees, then killing their parents.

Patrick was sure that these events did take place from time to time, however, the book only documented one specific event. It happened in what is now nearby Craigsville, West Virginia. By the time of this event, whites and Indians had already been killing each other upon site for some time. A group of Indians came across a small dwelling while the man of the house was on a hunt. They supposedly bashed the head of an infant into a tree, then killed the mother.

Upon returning from his hunt and finding this scene, the man put together a small group of men and went on the hunt of the Indians. When they came upon them days later, sleeping under a rock ledge along a stream, they killed every last one of them.

Patrick could only imagine how happy these events made the establishment at the time. It would allow them to desecrate the entire population of the native inhabitants without having to form and more importantly, pay an army to do it. They played on people's two most motivating emotions; fear and greed. Fear of the Indians and greed for want of the land.

Patrick now understood why Grady's story was so important. He assumed the tragedy that Grady Haines had replayed before his eyes had taken place during these settlement days. So, the graves belonged to a couple Indian girls and their mother and the family of the folks who had settled the mountain. This part of the mystery had been solved.

Now however, what Patrick couldn't understand entirely was the curse. How to rid the land of the great curse that had afflicted so many over the years, to include his own daughter Samantha? For him to have carried the curse with him, off of this mountain top and to have it follow him through life as it did, in order to affect his daughter, the curse must have indeed been strong.

#

The hoot from an owl somewhere in the distance brought Patrick back to awareness. He had fallen asleep while reading and it was now dark. He looked out into the field and the girls were gone. He began to rise, when he realized that Samantha's doll was sitting on his lap.

"Bless her little heart," he said aloud. Trixie had actually done the right thing and left the doll with him. He knew how hard it was for her to do so. She loved the doll so much.

Patrick took his book and chair inside. He lit a small fire in the wood stove. Though the days were still temperate, it was now growing quite cold at night. He would need the warmth.

He sprawled his sleeping bag out on the couch in front of the wood stove. He made his way into the kitchen to grab a beer.

He opened the door to the refrigerator, stared at the cans, then closed the door. He was going to take Amy's advice. He was not going to drink tonight. He wasn't as much concerned with brushing over any details, now that he was done reading, but he wanted to stay sober. See what it was like. He decided to have his first sober night in quite some time. A series of sober nights, should he manage to be able to string some together, started with just that. The first one.

"Let me ride in the front seat this time, daddy," Samantha said as Patrick opened the back door of his car, prepared to strap her into her seat belt.

"But you don't weigh enough yet, honey," he said, knowing she wouldn't take 'no' for an answer. She rarely did. It was his own fault. He spoiled her so.

"It's only a few minutes, daddy. I won't tell mommy or the cops." She said this, tilting her chin into her chest while looking up with big doe eyes. She knew this is all it would take to get her way.

"Ok," Patrick agreed. "Just don't tell anyone. And don't get used to it. This is the only time until you are older, ok?"

"Ok, daddy. I promise!" she said, running around to the passenger side of the car.

Patrick strapped her in, got in the driver's seat and started home. They had gone to the grocery store, only two miles from home, to get a cake mix and some icing. Samantha wanted chocolate cake and as far as her father was concerned, whatever Samantha wanted, she got.

Driving down the road, Samantha played with the radio knobs. "Is this how you do it?" she asked, hitting the seek button.

"Yes, honey. If you don't like the song that's on, just hit it again."

Samantha skipped through several stations, all playing commercials, before settling on a talk radio show.

"You don't want to listen to that, do you honey?" he asked. The voice of Sean Hannity, enraged with what he DECLARED to be the latest attack against the American people by the liberal, left winged establishment blared from the speakers.

"What's a liberal?" Samantha asked. "Why are they so evil?"

"They're not, honey," he told her. "They just have different views than this guy and he makes a lot of money to try to prove them wrong."

"Are you a liberal, daddy?"

"No, honey."

"What are you?"

"I'm somewhere in the middle, honey. Just like the majority of people. This is probably a conversation for when you are older."

He bent forward and started adjusting the radio station. He blew through several channels playing commercials, looking for suitable music for his seven year old daughter.

"Daddy! Look out!" she screamed in terror.

The sound of brakes squealing and the crashing of glass is all he heard. That and a "pop." When his car stopped spinning, the first thing he did was reach over for Samantha to make sure she was ok.

"Samantha?" he asked. "Samantha!" he yelled.

The airbag had ejected from the dash and broken her neck. She sat there, motionless and empty of life, her doe eyes open, staring directly at him, lifeless, her little chin tilted on her chest.

\#

"Samantha!" he woke with a start. He was covered in sweat. All was dark around him.

His hands, his entire body was trembling. It took him a minute to remember where he was. He wasn't in Virginia. He was in his cabin on top of Fork Mountain, outside of Richwood, West Virginia. He was sitting up now on his couch.

The fire in the stove had burned out. The room was cold. The sweat on his skin made him even colder. He checked his watch by the light of the indiglo and saw that it was 3:32 a.m.

He spun his feet around until they hit the floor then dropped his head into his hands, sobbing uncontrollably.

"Get yourself together," he said, trying to talk himself into calming down.

Deciding to get busy, he put another log in the wood stove. He moved the ashes around and blew on the few embers that remained and brought the fire back to life, making sure not to catch his cast on fire. He made his way to the refrigerator in the kitchen and got a beer.

"If this is what sobriety means, I want no part of it," he said. "I'd rather not feel if all I feel is bad." Saying this, he drew the can to his lips and drank half its contents in one giant gulp.

He sat there, staring at the fire, drinking his beer. He decided he would call the therapist Elizabeth had mentioned. He knew he wasn't crazy as far as seeing ghosts were concerned. He'd already had enough proof of that. He thought it might be a good idea to talk to someone about the dreams. About his drinking. About his depression that he no longer denied he had. And then there was…

…the graves…

The voice. Just as he thought of it he heard it again.

…of the babes…

He didn't even waste his time looking for anyone. He knew no one was there. Instead, he went to the refrigerator and got another beer.

"I don't know who you are," he said. "And I don't know what you're trying to tell me, but you can't drive me crazy. I'm already crazy. Why don't you just show yourself?"

Nothing happened. No one appeared. He knew his attempt was futile but he figured it was worth the effort just the same.

Several beers later he had relaxed enough to go back to sleep. He had that nice, "three beer buzz" though it took him five to reach it. He had forgotten the dream, or at least it's feeling of reality. He hoped it would be the last one but he had every reason to believe it would not be.

#

After a quick breakfast with his mother, Patrick made his way to the library to let Heather know what he had gathered from reading the book and to get the contact info on Elizabeth's friend the shrink. His mother showed her pleasure in his decision to at least talk to someone.

"So what did you find out?" Heather said in a whisper while he was booting up his laptop at a table in the back of the library.

"I learned lots of history," he said. "I think I can explain the visions Grady saw on the hill."

Patrick told Heather everything he had read in the book that pertained to their dilemma on top of Fork Mountain. She listened intently and hung on every word.

"So now what?" she asked.

"For now, I'm going to appease my sister and mother and go see a shrink in Summersville. Why don't you and Caleb come up again this weekend and we'll brainstorm."

"You know the deal," she said. "As long as we're outta there by dark."

"It's a deal then," he chuckled. He began checking emails while Heather got back to her duties at the library.

#

At one o'clock in the afternoon Patrick found himself sitting in the office of Byron Blevins at the Department of Social Services offices in Summersville. When he had called Blevins that morning he had agreed to see him that afternoon. Elizabeth had been talking to Blevins about her brother and he wanted to get him in as quickly as he could.

"So what is going on?" Blevins asked, his thin wired glasses resting on the bridge of his nose. He was kicked back in his big leather chair behind his desk. Patrick was seated on the other side.

"I lost my daughter about a year and a half ago," Patrick said.

"Yes," said Blevins, thoughtfully. "Your sister told me about that when it happened. How do you feel about that?"

Patrick could tell by this first exchange of words that the guy was a quack. By looking around the office, seeing all the books, the degrees on the wall, Patrick could tell that Blevins had spent more time with his nose in books chasing higher degrees than he had dealing with people.

Patrick, a former salesman, had learned years ago how to control a conversation. He determined instantly to do it today. He knew he'd get no real help from this man but that it would please his sister and mother that he had come. Blevins asking him how losing his daughter "made him feel" was all the proof he needed that his time would otherwise be wasted.

One of the greatest sales lessons Patrick had ever received was from a retired software engineer salesman he had met in his travels. The man had taught him the "whip" method of conversation control. He had told him that just as a lion tamer uses a whip to control a beast, a person could use a similar whip, a whip in the shape of a question mark, to control any conversation. Ask open ended questions so people cannot answer with a yes or a no. Answer questions with questions.

The political master of this had been Sir Winston Churchill. When asked once by a reporter if it was true that he always answered questions with another question, Churchill was reported to have said, "Now, who told you that?"

"How would something like that make you feel?" Patrick said, cracking the whip.

"Well," Blevins began. "I don't have children. My wife and I are waiting until we are ready."

"When will you be ready?" Patrick asked.

"Well, we're just now turning forty. My wife just finished her Phd. and I'm still working on my dissertation."

Blevins was confirming, without knowing it, the opinions Patrick had already formed of him.

"What is your dissertation on?" Patrick asked, gripping even tighter on the whip.

"It has to do with behavioral responses to unfamiliar stimulus after forming condition responses to conditioned stimulus."

"That sounds interesting," Patrick said, with a slight pause, allowing Blevins to think he would be able to ask the next question. Just as he opened his mouth to do so, Patrick spoke again. "What has brought you to this field of study?"

"Think for a minute about Pavlov's dog," Blevins began, now in full lecture mode. Patrick knew his job was done. "What would happen, if instead of ringing a bell in anticipation of salivation, you started blowing a horn? Would the dog still salivate? How long would it take for the dog to figure out that the rules of the game had been changed?"

Blevins filled the rest of the hour talking about his theories and his dissertation. Though not interested at all, Patrick paid very close attention, so when the time came for him to speak, which was very rare, he knew exactly what question to ask next, how to crack the whip, to keep Blevins talking about himself and off of any topics pertaining to him.

"This session went really well," Blevins said at the end of the hour. "I wish we had more time but I'm seeing someone else. We should schedule for next week."

"That would be great," Patrick said. "I feel this went well too. I'm glad I took my sister up on her suggestion to come see you. I feel so much better already."

Patrick left with an appointment for the same day and time the following week. It would be more of a nuisance and waste of his time to come, as he would do the exact same thing to Blevins at each appointment that he had done today. He knew though, that it would keep his family off his back, buying him time to figure out what exactly it was he could do to help the girls on top of the mountain. He left the office, smiling.

20

"I swear, I don't see anyone out there but Caleb," Heather said, staring across the field. She and Patrick were sitting by the picnic table in front of the cabin while Caleb played with the ghosts of the girls.

"They're there," Patrick said. "I see them."

It was now Saturday and Heather and Caleb had come back to Patrick's for another cook out and afternoon of fresh, mountain air, just as Heather had agreed to do earlier in the week at the library.

"I wish I could see them," she said.

"I'm glad you can't."

"Why?"

"Because for you to be able to do so, something tragic would have had to have happened to you."

"I wonder what happened to Grady Haines? Why could he see them?"

Patrick relayed the story to Heather that Bill Hammonds had told him, about Grady witnessing his mother kill his father and his uncle when he was a child.

"I didn't tell you before we met with Haines because I didn't want you to have any preconceived notions that he was indeed crazy. I'm sure seeing that as a young child could lead to insanity. I don't think it drove him crazy though. But I'm sure it is what "broke" him though, enabling him to see the spirits later in life."

"It makes sense," she said, rising to refill her glass with cold water taken from the mountain spring a few yards out in the woods from the cabin. It was better than any purified, bottled water she had ever had. "So it seems this curse can attach itself to people, follow them."

"I've had the exact same thoughts," Patrick said in a stern manner. "I think it attached itself to me and caused Samantha's disappearance."

"I wonder if it followed me?" she said. "Could that be why Caleb is blind?"

"Perhaps," Patrick said. "It seems only to affect girls but maybe that is just with death. Maybe Caleb suffered a little from your single night up here in high school."

Heather shuttered at the thought, turning now to return to her seat.

"What have you put together after reading that book? We now know WHY what happened, happened. If only we could figure out what knowing has to do with solving the problem?"

"I know," Patrick said, still pondering the riddle himself.

"What could you possibly do to make something like that right?" she said, now sitting again, sipping her water.

"It might sound crazy," Patrick began. "I mean, all of this would sound crazy to anyone, but I kinda think perhaps the old Shaman simply wants an apology."

"An apology?" Heather said, puzzled.

"Yeah," Patrick said. "I mean, after all this time, what more could you do? He and his warriors obviously took justice into their own hands. Who knows how many other tragedies they had befall them. This area probably got pretty saturated with white settlers around that time. Heck, their entire race would disappear within the next century, confined to a few reservations way out west in the rainy Pacific Northwest. The specific tribes of this area I'm sure were wiped out entirely."

"Yeah," Heather said, thinking of these facts. "I guess you're right."

"I can't figure out why I've never seen him, the Shaman," Patrick said. "If I could just talk to him, let him know that I know what happened."

"Have any of the girls ever talked about him?" Heather said, head motioning to the field where she still only saw Caleb.

"No. None of them have ever mentioned it. I think Amy would be the only one old enough to be able to have a conversation with me about it."

"When was the last time you saw her?" Heather asked.

"Earlier this week. She was keeping an eye on me and the girls while I read the book."

"Do you think she can protect you?" Heather really didn't know what questions to ask. She believed in all the ghosts and events Patrick had been seeing and experiencing, but since she herself never saw any of them she was still somewhat in the dark.

"No," he said. "At least I don't think so. She sure didn't show up to protect me the night I got my butt kicked," he said this, raising his broken hand, still in a cast. His face had cleared up quite a bit, save for a yellowish bruise below his left eye. "When I see her again I'll talk to her about this."

Patrick and Heather sat in silence, staring into the field. To Heather it looked like Caleb was playing with nuts. Patrick, however, saw that the girls were putting objects into the little boy's hands.

"This is an acorn," Sarah said. "Feel how sharp it is on the end?"

"This is a hickory nut," Amelia said, replacing the acorn. "It feels like a golf ball. The squirrels love these."

Trixie sat on the ground beside them, Samantha's doll sitting beside her. To Heather, it looked like the doll was simply lying in the field close to Caleb.

As they sat and watched two different sites, Patrick noticed movement just beside his left foot. He glanced down to see a blue crayfish emerging from its hole. He looked up instantly and saw that clouds were rolling in.

"We have to get out of here," he said with excitement, rising to his feet.

"What is it?" Heather asked, concerned.

"A storm's coming! You and Caleb can't be up here!"

"Is HE coming?" Heather asked, now rising to her feet as well.

"Yes!"

Patrick and Heather ran into the field. Heather grabbed Caleb, scaring him briefly, and began running with him to Patrick's truck.

"Girls!" Patrick said. "I think he's coming. I have to get Heather and Caleb off the hill. Go to wherever it is that you go when he comes!"

"Ok," Sarah said. "We have a place where he's never found us."

"Can I take the baby?" Trixie asked.

"Yes, honey!" Patrick said. "Take the baby. Just make sure you bring her back. Go now though, don't waste any time!"

Patrick ran to catch up with Heather and Caleb. Heather looked back just in time to see the doll disappear into the woods as if it were riding the wind.

"Oh my God," she mumbled, strapping Caleb's seat belt on him in the back seat.

"Get in!" Patrick said loudly, waving with his hands.

He got in himself, started the truck and began heading off of the mountain.

"I hope they'll be ok," Heather said.

"They'll be fine," Patrick said, looking in his rear view mirror. He could see a patch of fog materializing by where they had been sitting just before he dropped over the hill and the area was out of site. "There's not much I can do to help them in my present state anyway. They've been fine for the past thirty years before I got up here."

Patrick drove to the foot of Fork Mountain. He turned the truck around to face up the hill. They sat in silence as they witnessed the storm clouds and the rain they brought to the secluded little area. The rest of the sky, in all directions, was crystal blue. There wasn't a single cloud to be seen anywhere else. Ten minutes later the clouds disappeared as quickly as they had come.

"Is he gone?" Heather asked.

"I think so," Patrick said.

"I wonder who he is?" Heather asked.

"I have no clue, but I think that is a big piece of the puzzle."

"He's Amy's uncle," Caleb offered from the back seat. Patrick and Heather turned in unison to stare at the boy.

"How do you know that, honey?" Heather asked.

"My new friends told me."

Patrick and Heather just stared at each other. Now they knew who the ghost of the old man was. Now what they needed to know was why he tormented the girls, even in death. More than that, they needed to know how to stop him.

The next month passed relatively uneventfully. It was now mid October and fall was in the air. What had been a green mountain was now one scattered with reds, purples, yellows and oranges. Winds and rain had brought many leaves to the ground, carpeting Patrick's field in the various colors.

Patrick had enjoyed the company of the girls at his farm. Amy, though not with them all the time, made an appearance at least once a week. She always spoke in riddles. Patrick felt she was trying to steer him toward something but he knew not what. Perhaps she herself didn't know exactly where she was trying to lead him, hoping that his mind would ingest her ideas and come up with its own.

Patrick had tried to engage her in conversation about her uncle after Caleb's enlightenment on the subject. Every time Amy only grew nervous and would begin to leave, until finally Patrick dropped the subject. Her nervousness confirmed to him that this was indeed the ghost of her uncle, but again, he still had not put together all the reasoning as to his motives. He never drew closer to any conclusions on the man's actions during life, or why he had become such a part of the riddle in his death.

Having formed a generally good opinion of Phillip Ables years before, and having always felt apprehensive around Phillip's brother Pete, the thought that weighed mostly on his mind was that perhaps it was indeed Pete who had committed the hideous crimes on top of Fork Mountain in the past, Phillip being the one who took the rap. If only he could talk to Amy about it. If he could only get her take on the matter.

Patrick had continued seeing his new councilor Byron Blevins on a weekly basis. Each time was the same as his first visit. Blevins would ask a question or two then Patrick would take control of the whip, in the form of his own line of questioning and have the councilor fill the hour with his own talk. It wasn't helping Patrick in any degree, except for keeping his sales skills sharp, should he ever decide to go back into that line of work. It was also keeping his mother and sister off his back. He did feel though as if some day he should seek real help as he could never rid his nights of the nightmares. He still drank himself to sleep most nights.

Patrick and Heather had solidified their relationship, the old love they held for each other many years before having been rekindled. She and Caleb still visited his cabin on the weekends, when the weather permitted, but they were always sure to get off of the mountain before dark. Patrick however, had spent several nights at Heather's house, not making it back to his own place until the following day. This seemed to be of considerable interest to the girls and the object of much teasing from Amy.

One such October afternoon, in which Patrick had spent most of his time with Heather and Caleb had now come to a close. He spent the evening having a few beers on the porch, to the disappointment of Amy, while watching the rest of the girls play in the yard.

He was pleased with how far Trixie had come in changing her behaviors. Though she always seemed to be up to some sort of trickery, often at the consternation of Sarah and Amelia, even Amy, she had never taken Samantha's doll or anything else to his knowledge. He was pleased too that the ghost of Pete Ables had not re-visited him. This last fact he couldn't explain but he was happy about it nonetheless.

After the girls walked up to the top of the hill to retire for the evening, Patrick went into his cabin to do the same. He lit a small fire on in the wood stove, staring at its flickering flames and drifted off to sleep.

#

Patrick was walking with Samantha. They were holding hands, heading up the hill to the graves. Once there, they noticed all the things Trixie had taken in the past. They were piled up yet again on top of several of the unmarked graves.

"Why is my doll up here, Daddy?" Samantha asked.

"Trixie must have taken it again, honey. I've told her not to take it out of the cabin."

"Why are there beer cans and cookies up here?" Samantha asked.

"For some reason, Trixie brings everything she takes from me up here to the graves. I don't know why."

"Maybe she's trying to tell you something, daddy," Samantha said. "And why are you drinking beer? You never drank before."

"What would she be trying to tell me honey?" he asked. He felt shame in regard to her question about his drinking.

Samantha walked over to her doll that was lying on top of one of the graves. She picked it up, turning again to face her father. Just as she did, Patrick noticed a blue craw crab make its way out of a hole beside her feet.

"Honey!" he shouted. "We have to run!"

"Why, Daddy?" she asked.

Just then two hands, those belonging to Pete Ables, came up through the grave, grabbed Samantha by the ankles and started pulling her into the ground.

#

"No!" he awoke with a start, sweating and shaking.

···the graves···

The voice came in almost a soothing tone. It reminded him where he was.

···of the babes"

That's it!" Patrick said aloud. "Why have I not thought of it before?"

He got up quickly, grabbed his battery powered Coleman lantern and headed outside. He made his way quickly to his out building and undid the combination lock, still the numbers of Samantha's birthday. He hadn't had the heart to change it.

Inside the shed, he grabbed his shovel. He turned quickly and made his way back outside. The lantern lit the way for him as he began to make his way up the hill. He was going to the graves, lantern and shovel in hand. He had some digging to do on this dark, October night.

Patrick reached the graves out of breath and covered with sweat. He had gotten in much better shape, having hiked quite a bit through the hills since his arrival this past summer, but he had climbed the hill at a quicker pace than usual. He was a man on a mission.

Patrick broke ground on one of the graves. Why had this idea evaded him for so long? Respect for the dead perhaps?

He had always wondered why no one had ever found the bodies of the girls who had gone missing years before. Where better to hide bodies than in graves that already existed? People would walk by them, having been aware of their existence, and never pay them a second thought.

Why had Trixie taken all of her stolen goods to the graves? Was she indeed trying to lead him to her body? The bodies of the other girls? It had been so obvious, yet he never thought of it even though the mysterious voice that had visited him repeatedly had given him the answer.

Patrick worked frantically by the light of the lantern. He was wishing he had brought a small hand saw as well. Tree roots had grown into the grave, making it difficult to dig. He was so frantic he didn't want to take the time to return to the shed for another tool. He stomped forcefully on the shovel, using it as a blade to break the roots.

Three feet into the grave he started hitting rock. He kept working, sweating profusely as he did. He was not going to allow roots or rocks to interrupt his mission. Four feet down, he hit something he thought was rock but was not. It crumbled too easily under the weight of his shovel.

He moved the lantern closer, placing it inside the hole. He got on his knees to inspect what he had hit. Sure enough, it was a skull. It was a skull small enough to be that of a child. But what child? Would the skull of one of the Indian girls from so long ago still be intact?

He placed the skull at the edge of the grave and kept digging. Only minutes later he hit another. Getting back on his knees, he saw that this too was a small skull, no doubt belonging to a child.

"That's it!" he said. "There is more than one body in this grave!"

Patrick moved to another grave. He dug with the same fervor that he had before. He fought through rocks and roots and found another skull. This too was a small, child sized skull. He placed it with the others and kept digging. A couple minutes later, he found yet another skull. This one was still attached, or at least still laying close to what appeared to be a spine. He dug around this part of the skeleton with his hands to reveal a light brown article of clothing. He pulled it out and held it to the light. The light allowed his eyes to make out a patch. It was a girl scout patch!

That is how the killer had done it! He killed the girls then buried them in the unmarked graves.

"Hold it right there, Pat!" the voice came from above him.

Patrick looked up, lifting the lantern, to see Phillip Ables standing only feet away, .45 in hand. The pistol was being pointed right at him.

"How could you do this?" Patrick said, incredulously. "How could you do such a thing to such innocents?"

"You just back outta that hole nice and slow," Ables said. "Put down that shovel and I'll save either of us having to make another grave." His eyes were cold.

Patrick eased out of the whole as the old man had ordered. He sat on the ground, laying the shovel beside him.

"You killed them!" Patrick said. "You killed all of them. You'll never get away with this now. I've found them and I'll have the state police up here in the morning!"

"I aint goin' back to prison!" Ables yelled, anger in both his tone and his eyes.

"Use your head, Ables. You don't have time to get rid of my body if you pull that trigger. People know I'm up here. They'll come looking for me. And I've upset your little hiding place here."

"Now you sit there and keep your mouth shut!" the old man demanded. "I don't wanna pull this trigger but I will if I have to! I ain't killed but one man since Korea, but I'll kill you if I have to!"

Patrick was on the losing end of the .45. He did as Ables said. He sat in silence as the old man began to speak.

#

"Yeah, you're a smart one," Ables began. "I always knew that. I can't believe you figured this out before I did though."

"Figured what out?" Patrick asked, confused. "Where you hid the bodies? Had you forgotten?"

"I didn't hide no bodies nowhere," he said. "My brother hid these bodies."

"So you were both in on it?"

"I take it you don't know the meaning of the phrase 'shut up,' do you?"

Patrick gulped, biting his tongue and remaining silent.

"Now I'm gonna lower this here .45 but I'm hangin' on to it," Ables said, doing as he said he would. "You listen, hear me out, and we aint gonna have no troubles. You get jumpy though, and though I ain't as fast as I used to be, these here bullets aint slowed down none."

Patrick remained silent. He figured he'd hear the man out. Listen to his story.

"My brother was one twisted son of a gun," Ables began. "I never felt comfortable around him even as a kid. Why, he was mean to animals. He'd go huntin' and I swear he'd intentionally wound a deer just so he could cut its throat with his knife. And he enjoyed doin' it! He laughed while he did it!"

Patrick was disgusted. He himself, when he hunted in his younger days, would never take a shot at an animal unless he was certain he'd hit the "kill zone," a vital organ, causing the animal to die quickly without suffering.

"But I'd never have suspected he'd carry that over to hurtin' kids when he got older," the old man continued. "Had I known he was doin' it, I'd have killed him long before I did. I would have never gone to prison, these girls wouldn't have gotten killed and I'd still have my Amy."

"What are you talking about?" Patrick asked, thinking he was finally catching on. He just wanted more clarity.

"I'm tryin' to tall ya," Ables said. "Just listen!"

Phillip Ables relayed the story of his brother Pete. He said that in the late sixties, he'd disappear for days. He'd say he was going hunting and camping. Phillip had never understood why he would need to go elsewhere to camp. They lived on top of the mountain, in the middle of the woods already. He would go though, and not be seen for days at a time.

Phillip said that Pete always acted weird when news would come out about one of the children who had gone missing. He started avoiding going into town as much as possible.

At the time, Phillip was unable to put two and two together. Once he did though, he asked Pete point blank if he had any involvement in the disappearances of the girls. Pete turned defensive, denying any involvement whatsoever.

Less than a week after Phillip had asked him about it, the state police came to the mountain top and arrested him, Phillip. They arrested him on charges of kidnapping and murder, though the bodies had never been found.

"That worthless bag of trash testified in court that I had told him I killed the girls and burned the bodies," Ables said. "It was nothing but a lie, but enough of one to put me away for twenty years. I knew then, that Pete was the one responsible.

I even tried to tell it when I got on the stand, but no one would listen."

Patrick was calm now. He believed the story Phillip Ables was telling him. He had always liked and trusted the man. He never knew him to lie. Pete had always given him the creeps.

"So your brother got away with it?" Patrick asked when Phillip took a pause.

"He got away with it and he did it again!" the old man said.

"But there were no more missing children," Patrick said. "Not that my research turned up."

"There was one more," Ables said.

"Who?"

"My daughter, Amy," he said.

"When I got out of prison and came back up here, Pete wanted to act like the previous twenty years hadn't happened. Like everything was just fine and dandy. I wasn't gonna let it go though."

"I kept badgerin' him about it. He had taken to drinkin' heavy. One night, I was on his case about the murders after he'd had a fifth of Jack Daniels. He just started laughin' and told me that Amy never drowned."

"What happened?" Patrick asked

"He killed her!" Ables said. "He went on and on about how pretty she'd turned out to be. Seems he tried to have his way with her, his own niece who he'd raised himself after I went away! She resisted and he killed her! Strangled her, he told me. They were swimming' down at the swimming' hole at the time. He started screaming for help, and made it look like she'd drowned."

That was why Amy didn't live at the graves with the rest of the girls. She had not been killed nor buried there. She had been buried at the Richwood Cemetery on Rhododendron Drive. That would explain why Patrick had met her at the swimming hole as well.

"What did you do when he told you that?" Patrick said, mesmerized by the story.

"You see this here?" Ables asked, pulling the pistol back up. "Directly I went and got this here .45 and I blew a hole in him."

"Where did you put the body?" Patrick asked.

"Under the floorboards of my cabin," he said. "No one ever asked any questions. He'd stayed outta town about as much as he could anyway, especially after he killed Amy."

Silence settled over the two men at the graves. Phillip had told the entire story. Patrick let it settle in his mind. He believed the man..

"I'm just afraid," Ables finally spoke, "that if they come up here and find these graves I'll go back to prison."

"That doesn't have to happen," Patrick said.

"What do you mean?" Ables asked, looking up, cheer now in his tone. Perhaps his worst fear was not going to come to fruition.

"They've given up looking for these girls long ago," Patrick said. "Sure, the families might have some relief if they found them, but that would do you no good. There'd be too many questions. Even though Pete was a scoundrel, if they knew that you killed him they 'd probably prosecute you anyway. That is how our beloved justice system works. There is no justice."

"I know that all too well," Ables said.

"Perhaps for now it is best to just let old bones lie," Patrick said. "What we need to do is more important anyway."

"How's that?" Ables asked.

"You know what goes on up here," Patrick said. "You've known about it for a long time. You've even tried to warn me."

"That's a fact," Ables said.

"Well, we have to figure out how to release the girls from your brother's abuses. That should be our focus."

"I've been focusing on that for a long time," Ables said. "I just haven't been able to figure out how."

"We'll figure that out together," Patrick said.

"I appreciate it Pat, really I do."

"There's something else you'll appreciate knowing," Patrick added.

"What's that?"

"I've seen Amy. I've talked to her on several occasions."

"Really?"

"Yeah. She said to let you know that she knows you didn't do what you were accused of doing. She worries about you. But she wanted you to know that she knew you were innocent."

Phillip Ables hung his head and wept.

"Thanks for coming to pass out candy while I take Caleb trick-or-treating," Heather said as she held Caleb's hand on her front porch. Patrick sat on the porch swing, a large salad bowl of candy in his lap. Caleb was dressed like Captain Jack Sparrow from "Pirates of the Caribbean."

"Where else would I be tonight?" Patrick asked with a nervous chuckle. "Up at my place? Who knows who might show up tonight of all nights."

"I know," Heather said, a chill running down her spine. "We'll be back in about an hour."

"Take your time," Patrick said. "You are one mean looking pirate," he directed toward Caleb.

"You will always remember this as the day you ALMOST caught Captain Jack Sparrow," the boy said with a giggle.

Heather and Caleb were off. The first group of trick-or treaters made their way to the porch. Patrick put a bite sized snickers bar into the bag of a werewolf, the jack 'o lantern bucket of a vampire, and the pillowcase of a cute little princess.

"Thank you," the princess said, reminding him of his own little princess who had disappeared over two years before.

"You are very welcome, Sweetie," he said, the girl's crooked smile giving a tug at his heart.

The hour went by quickly and Patrick passed out almost all of the candy, saving a few of the snickers bars for himself. This had always been his favorite candy.

Heather returned with Caleb who had a huge bag full of candy.

"Wow!" Patrick said. "I hope you have lots of toothpaste."

"They always give me more candy than the rest of the kids," Caleb said.

"Sometimes others taking pity isn't a bad thing, is it?" His mother said.

"It's not that," Caleb said defensively. "I always have the best costume."

Heather and Patrick both laughed at the boy's wit.

"So what are you going to do now?" Heather asked Patrick.

"I guess I'm going home," he said.

"Are you sure you want to be up there tonight?" she asked. "You are more than welcome to stay here."

"I appreciate it," he told her. "I think I should be up there though. If there is any fact based on the reasons we celebrate All Hallows Eve, perhaps more will be revealed to me and we can get all of this behind us."

"Yeah," Heather said. "I hope so. I just hope nothing bad happens."

"I've already figured out I can't hurt him," Patrick said in regard to the ghost of Pete Ables. He rubbed his right hand for effect. It was now out of its cast and healed for the most part. "I can hide the girls though then draw attention to myself. I think I can evade him."

"I would go with you if I thought it would do any good," Heather said. "But Caleb…" she trailed off, looking toward her son, visible through the glass door. He was sitting on the living room floor digging through his candy.

"I know," Patrick said. "Don't worry about it. I have my cell and if I need any help I'll call you. Make sure you sleep with your phone by your bed tonight."

"I always do," she said.

#

Patrick's head lights cut through the darkness like razor blades as he headed up Fork Mountain. All the trick-or-treaters and their parents had disappeared with the town behind him. Straight up into darkness he continued to climb on this unseasonably warm, Halloween night.

He hadn't told Heather, not wanting to cause extra worry, but he and Phillip Ables had a plan. They were going to confront the ghost of Pete Ables. What better night to run into him than on All Hallows Eve?

Patrick had taken the time to explain all of his thoughts on the subject to Phillip. He had told him of his visit to Grady Haines and of all the things he learned while there. He told him how he agreed with Grady that a great curse had been put on the land due to the actions of the settlers, years before, against the daughter and grand daughters of the Indian shaman.

Patrick drove a little slower than usual once he'd passed the final house in Handle Factory Hollow. The multi-colored leaves covered the road, their reflections from his head lights giving off an eerie glow.

He drove with the window down, enjoying the night air, thinking also that if there were anything lurking in the woods just off of the side of the road, his lowered windows would allow him to hear it.

He finally reached his cabin, having seen nothing on the road. He grabbed his flashlight from the passenger seat of his truck and used it to make his way to the door. Clouds had rolled in on his way up the mountain and it was now dark as pitch. The scent of a coming rain was in the air. Though this is ordinarily what Patrick hoped would not happen, tonight he had hoped that it would. He could only imagine the blue crayfish starting to crawl out of mysteriously appearing holes in the field.

Making his way into the cabin, Patrick quickly turned on a kerosene lantern he had sitting on the end table at the end of the couch in the living room. He didn't want to start the gasoline powered generator. He didn't want any artificial noise at all this evening. He was not being any more superstitious than he normally was, but he was very aware of the date. He could smell the coming rain outside. If there were anyone or anything that was going to make a sound he wanted to be able to hear it. He didn't want the sound drowned out by the generator.

Patrick fought the urge to have a beer. He wanted to be completely sober this evening. At least until after he and Phillip made an honest effort to confront the ghost of Pete Ables.

He lit a small fire in the wood stove and sat back and watched the flames. As they flickered, he drifted off, not into a deep sleep, but enough to allow his mind to work on its own. He was not controlling his thoughts. He would be meeting with Phillip Ables at the grave site soon. He knew he couldn't rest for long. But sleep came upon him.

#

Phillip Ables sat in his cabin which was dimly lit by a kerosene lantern. He held his .45, not really sure of what good it would do, and stared at the picture of Amy on the mantle.

"I'm gonna make it alright tonight," he said. "I'm gonna make it alright."

He had been even more emotional as of late, Patrick having informed him that he had been communicating with Amy. Her ghost, the only one on the mountain he had never seen, was what had kept him going. It was the reason behind all those late nights sitting in the woods above Patrick's cabin.

He had been seeing the ghosts of the little girls ever since getting out of prison. He hoped that someday he would finally be able to see Amy's ghost. He wanted to talk to her, tell her he hadn't done what he had been convicted of doing.

It lightened his agony, knowing that Amy already knew. He just wished that he could talk to her himself. He hadn't seen her since she was four years old.

Phillip stood up and put his gun holster around his waist. His magazine held nine rounds and he kept another twenty around his waist. He knew it was more than he'd ever need at any given time, but he would rather have too many rounds than not enough.

He turned the wick on the lantern so low that it barely glowed. He wanted to have a little light left in his cabin when he returned. If he returned. He headed for the door to meet up with Patrick.

TAP TAP TAP

Phillip heard the sound coming from the middle of the room. Expecting a mouse he turned, pistol raised, to see that nothing was there.

TAP TAP TAP

The noise came again. He looked down and saw the floor boards begin to shake. The tapping grew louder and a nail shot up through the boards as if it had been shot out of a gun. Phillip cocked the hammer to his .45 and steadied it low to the floor.

#

It was Saturday morning. Like so many Saturday mornings Patrick tried to sleep in just a little longer. He remained in bed, hoping he could buy a little more time. He heard his bedroom door squeak as it opened and he knew he would not be able to get the extra rest he had hoped for.

Samantha tiptoed through his bedroom. She put her face right against his and began to whisper.

"Wake up daddy, it's time to wake up," she said. "Wake up daddy."

#

Patrick's eyes opened. He was calm, his heart rate low. He had hoped to see Samantha's beautiful face when he opened his eyes, but all he saw was the flickering flame in the wood stove at his cabin on top of Fork Mountain.

"Uh oh!" he said aloud, realizing he was supposed to be meeting Phillip Ables at the graves at this time. He rose to his feet, still fully dressed, grabbed his battery powered lantern and went outside.

He stood on the porch for a second, gauging the atmosphere of his surroundings. The sky was completely cloud covered, not a star in sight. Though it had been warm earlier, the temperature was dropping quickly. A chill wind was picking up from the east.

He stepped off the porch to go to the graves. Phillip should be on his way to the graves as well if he weren't there yet. Patrick heard nothing out of the ordinary, stopping every few feet to listen.

He crossed his field in this manner. He'd walk ten paces then stop to listen. Walked ten paces, then stopped to listen.

He began walking again after one such stop, when on his second step he heard a loud "crunch." He held his lantern close to the ground to see what he feared he would see. He had crushed a small blue crayfish. As he wiped the small, gooey carcass from his boot heel, he heard a shot from a .45 ring out through the woods above him.

Patrick hurried to the top of the hill to the graves. He hoped that nothing bad had befallen his old friend because he himself had not been where he said he would be when he said he would be there. The shot had sounded further away than the graves, so Patrick was confused as to what exactly was happening.

Upon reaching the graves he saw that no one was there. It was now raining. There were blue crayfish crawling on the unmarked head and footstones of the graves.

"Philip!" he yelled. "Philip!" No answer.

He heard another shot. He could tell it was coming from the direction of Phillip's cabin. He quickly began making his way down the trail in that direction.

#

"That will do you no good now brother!" the ghost of Pete Able's laughed after Phillip had taken his second shot. Had the evil brother still been alive, the bullet would have blown a hole clean through him, as Phillip Ables was a crack shot. "You can't kill what's already dead!"

"You listen here you evil dog! You go on back to hell where you belong!"

"But it's so much more enjoyable here!" The ghost said before taking a swing at his living brother.

The punch caught Philip on the chin and sent him straight to the ground. He lay there, unconscious, but still alive.

"You should have kept your mouth shut and left well enough alone," the ghost of Pete Ables said, towering over his unconscious brother. He had taken up the poker from the fireplace and now held it high above his head, ready to crash it down on the skull of his brother.

"Stop!" Patrick yelled. He had finally reached the cabin, sweaty and out of breath, but apparently just in time.

"You!" the ghost bellowed. "You want more of me yourself, do you?" Pete dropped the poker and started making his way to the door where Patrick was standing, hands on his knees, still catching his breath.

Run! Patrick thought. Run!

With this thought, he started to turn to do just that. Then he thought better of it, knowing Phillip was laid out on the floor. He turned and instead made his way into the cabin.

But before he could bend over to check on his friend, Pete Ables grabbed the poker he had just dropped, raised it high and struck Patrick across the back.

Patrick let out an agonizing scream and dropped to the floor. He could see that his scream had done a bit of good, waking Philip, who looked like he had no clue where he was. He probably didn't.

Pete raised the poker again and brought it crashing down toward Patrick. He was able to get out of the way this time, the poker's sharp prong sticking into the floorboards.

Patrick noticed movement out of the corner of his eyes. He glanced toward the movement, by the fireplace, and saw Amy standing there. She mouthed the word "run." She shooed him away with her hand.

Patrick took the hint. He knew Philip was alive and he trusted Amy would care for him. He made his way out the door and started running toward the graves.

#

As Patrick ran the rain began to come down harder. Thunder boomed in the sky and streaks of lightning lit his way. He had dropped his lantern at Phillip's cabin, more concerned with getting out of there when he left than picking it up.

His pace was slowed by darkness, yet the lightning was coming so regularly now, every few seconds, that he could see enough of the path sprawled out in front of him during each flash that he could comfortably move by faith during the dark. One thing was for sure, he wasn't going to stop and allow Pete Ables to catch up to him.

Patrick finally reached the graves. As much as his natural instincts told him to run, his mind told him to stop, hold his ground. This was the night that he and Phillip had decided to confront the evil spirit of Pete Ables. So far, nothing about tonight had gone as planned, but Patrick was to remain determined.

He turned slowly, his heart continuing to pound heavily even though he had stopped running. It pounded now as a result of fear, not exertion. The next lightning flash revealed what he hoped yet at the same time feared he would see. The ghost of Pete Ables, fire poker in hand, was coming around the bend.

"It stops tonight, Pete!" Patrick yelled, sounding more confident that he really was.

"Yes," Pete said. "It ends tonight. You'll be in my way no longer once I rid this mountain top of you then go back and finish off my brother!"

"I don't fear you!" Patrick said, again faking his confidence. "Go to hell and don't come back!"

"You're going to Hell!" Pete yelled, lunging forward, poker coming down toward Patrick's head.

Patrick side stepped out of the way. He slipped in the fresh mud but was able to catch himself on a tree before completely falling. He was fortunate to have done so. Obviously Pete Ables thought he would go straight to the ground and had aimed his next swing perfectly. It hit where Patrick would have landed.

Patrick jumped back a few feet, putting distance between him and the evil spirit of Pete Ables.

"I do not fear you!" he said again.

All this statement brought was more wrath and fury from Pete. He lunged forward and swung sideways at Patrick's head. Patrick ducked. He rose with an uppercut that would have caught Pete square in the jaw and sent him flying backward, but just as the night of their first fight, Patrick's fist went flying straight through him. The force of the punch, not being subdued by his fist stopping on Pete's body, sent him twisting sideways. He slipped in the mud again and this time was unable to catch himself. He fell straight to the ground.

Pete connected with his next swing of the poker. He caught Patrick on the back of his right calf, the poker's spike piercing into his skin and two inches into his muscle.

Patrick howled in pain. As Pete plucked the poker out of his leg and raised it again, Patrick did the best he could to crawl away. His efforts were in vain. The next fall of the poker caught him squarely in the back of his left calf. Both legs were now rendered useless.

Patrick managed to crawl forward, pulling himself to a sitting position with the help of an unmarked headstone on one of the graves.

"Stop!" Patrick pleaded. "What do you want?"

"I want you gone!" Pete said, coming down again with the poker. He was aiming for Patrick's head. Patrick tried to duck and managed somewhat, but still took the blow in his left shoulder. The poker dug two inches into his flesh. Patrick let out another howl.

Pete would not relent. He took the poker out of Patrick's flesh as quickly as he had implanted it. He raised it again and this time connected with Patrick's head when he brought it down hard.

The poker had been facing the wrong way to drive the spike into Patrick's head, perhaps the only reason the blow had not killed him. Patrick was knocked over, now lying on his side on the muddy earth. The rain came and smeared the blood that was spewing from his body all over him. Though the spike had not caught him, the blow from the poker still cut him and brought blood.

Patrick's vision was blurring. He looked up and could see Pete raising the poker again by the light of the lightning. He stuck up his arm to block the blow as best he could. It helped a little, but not much, as another forceful blow came crashing down. This one caught his hand, poker spike first, and went almost entirely through. There was enough force on the swing to cause him to hit himself in the face, busting his nose.

Patrick now felt light headed. He looked up toward Pete, doing his best to see the angle from which the next blow would come with the next streak of lightning. As the lightning came, he saw Pete, poker raised. He saw something else in the light this time too.

Sitting behind Pete was a horse. Sitting on top of the horse was an Indian shaman. The old shaman was watching everything.

"I'm sorry," Patrick mumbled.

"What was that?" Pete said. "Are you begging?"

"I'm sorry!" Patrick said, more volume in his voice. He was not directing this comment toward Pete. He was directing it toward the shaman.

Patrick's vision was going fast. However, he could still hear. In between the claps of thunder, he heard branches snapping as the horse drew closer.

The next lightning flash revealed the shaman directly behind Pete Ables. Ables turned to face the shaman.

"We're all sorry," Patrick said, mustering every bit of strength he had left to speak the words.

Out of what must have been his own sense of fear, Pete Ables dropped the poker to the ground. He stared speechless at the shaman on the horse.

The shaman mumbled something incoherent to Patrick then grabbed the ghost of Pete Ables by the hair of the head. Pete fought but could not resist. The strength of the shaman was supernatural. Even more so than Pete's own strength.

The next lighting flash allowed Patrick to see what followed. The shaman, never leaving the back of his horse, nor letting go of the hair of Pete Ables' head turned, took one giant leap, then disappeared into one of the graves.

Pete was gone. The rain began to stop. The lightning and thunder ceased. Patrick passed out in a pool of mud and his own blood.

Patrick was awakened the next morning by the sound of birds chirping and chipmunks rustling through dry leaves. He painfully opened his eyes, the first thing he saw being an unmarked tombstone.

He tried rising to his feet and found that he could not. He began crawling down the hill to his cabin. A fourth of the way down, finding that this means of travel would take him all day, he finally managed to pull himself to his feet by the use of a tree. He figured out a way to limp from tree to tree and again resumed his trek off of the hill.

He had to go slowly due to the pain he was in. He rested for at least a full minute each time he got to a new tree.

When he finally made his way to the field he saw Sarah standing outside his cabin, just in front of the porch.

"He's coming!" she yelled inside.

At that moment, Amelia and Trixie, Samantha's doll in hand, came outside. However, there was another little girl with them. From this distance he could not make out who she was. Seeing that the girls were coming to him, he sat in the field, waiting.

As the girls got closer, he began to make out who the other girl was. He rubbed his eyes to make sure that he was not dreaming. He wasn't. He was completely awake. The scene he saw before him was real. The girl that was coming through the field with the others was Samantha!

"Hi, Daddy," she said, once the girls reached him.

"Samantha?" he asked. "Is that really you?"

"Yes, Daddy," she said.

"Oh, honey," he said, taking her in his arms and giving her a giant hug. It was a hug he had longed to give her for more than two years.

"What happened to you, honey?" he asked, pulling back to look at her big brown eyes and her crooked smile. Tears were pouring down his face.

"I'm ok now daddy," she said. "That is all you need to know."

He took her answer as the best he'd get, the only one he needed and hugged her again.

After the hug, Samantha stood tall.

"Daddy," she said.

"Yes, honey?"

"I have to go now."

"Go where, honey?"

"I have to go back to Grandpa."

"Grandpa?" he said, confused.

"Yes," she said. "He is taking really good care of me, so don't worry about anything. We have lots of fun together."

"Ok," he said. "Will I get to see you again?"

"Not here," she said. "But don't worry. You will see me again and when you do it will feel like time hasn't passed. Then we'll always be together."

"I won't leave you again when that time comes, honey. I promise."

"I know you won't, daddy."

She leaned in to him when she saw him struggling to rise to give her another hug. She cherished the hug herself before parting.

"There are a couple things I want you to do for me, daddy," she said.

"Anything," he said.

"Stop treating yourself so badly."

"What do you mean, honey?"

"Stop drinking," she said. "It hurts me to know that you are doing that to yourself. It won't bring me back and it is only killing you. We will be together in time, but I don't want it to come too soon because of how you've been living."

Patrick looked down, his heart sinking.

"I'm not upset with you, daddy," Samantha said. "I just know it is killing you. It makes me sad to see you do it."

"Ok, honey," he said. "I'll stop. I promise."

"Good," she said in her old, bossy girl tone. 'Bossy Bessy Moo Cow' Patrick used to call her when she exhibited it.

"There's something else, daddy," she added.

"What's that, honey?"

"Stop blaming Mommy," she said. "It's not her fault. She blames herself and it doesn't do any good that you do too."

"I will, honey. I promise."

The two locked in another hug. The night before had been dreadful for Patrick but this morning, in spite of his pain, made it all worth it.

"Uh hum!" Trixie said from behind Samantha.

"Oh yeah," Samantha said. "There's one more thing."

"What's that, honey?"

"Trixie can have my doll."

Patrick glanced at Trixie. She was holding the doll tightly against her chest, twisting from side to side, a mischievous smile on her face.

"Ok, honey," he said. "Trixie can have your doll." This last part he said while facing Trixie. The mischievousness of her smile disappeared. Now she only smiled. It was a beautiful smile.

The girls helped steady Patrick to his feet then across the field to his house. Though he was in agonizing pain, he could tell that the overall atmosphere of the area had lifted. He could sense that the girls were all at peace. They had always been such sweet children but they had an invisible yet highly sensible aura of despair around them. This was no doubt due to the constant torment they dealt with at the hands of the ghost of Pete Ables. This aura was now gone as they would never have to deal with this again. Patrick had helped them and they in turn, through bringing Samantha to him for a proper goodbye, had helped him as well.

When they got to the porch, he sat down, wincing in pain as he did. It was a couple of minutes before he raised his head and turned out to face the field. When he finally did, he saw that the girls were gone. They had crossed over. He would never see them again. All that remained as proof of their existence was an aged cabbage patch doll lying in the grass that now took extra special meaning for Patrick. It had belonged to the two of the most special girls he had ever known.

Six months later

"Oh yes, I remember that time," Patrick spoke into the phone. "Remember the time she stuck her head with a thorn on a Bradford Pear tree going through the bushes to the neighbor's yard? I took her to the emergency room fearing she was going to bleed to death and the nurses all made fun of me? I had no clue that the head was 'very vascular' as they called it and that the slightest cut would bleed like crazy."

"Ok, Shannon," Patrick spoke into the phone after pausing to listen. "It was nice talking to you again too. Give me a call in a few days and let me know how everything is going down there in Mississippi."

He clicked off his cell phone and walked over to join the party. He had a big smile on his face, having enjoyed yet another conversation with his ex wife Shannon. They had come so far in rebuilding their friendship in the past several months.

"Happy six months anniversary to you. Happy six months anniversary to you. Happy six months anniversary dear Patrick. Happy six months anniversary to you!" the small group sang, standing over the picnic table in Patrick's field. A cake with a lit candle in the shape of the number six on top of it sat on the table.

"Thanks guys," he said humbly.

Heather had thrown together an impromptu six month sobriety party for Patrick. Philip Ables was there, as well as Ginny, Elizabeth, Caleb and Byron Blevins.

"I couldn't have done it without you guys," he said, picking up a knife to cut the cake.

Phillip Ables had also survived that dark Halloween night six months earlier. After Patrick had led the ghost of Pete Ables out of Phillip's cabin, Amy nursed her father back to health and had a talk with him. Neither Phillip nor Patrick had seen her since.

Patrick had heeded the requests of his little girl. He not only stopped drinking but called his ex wife Shannon to "make amends" as the twelve step program Blevins had recommended he join convinced him to do. He no longer blamed Shannon for Samantha's disappearance. He found that by releasing his hate and anger, it was much easier to go without a drink.

After finishing their cake, the adults all sat in their chairs drinking lemonade and chatting. They watched as Caleb entertained himself in the field which was now turning quite green again with the advent of spring. The trees around the field's edges were budding and Patrick had indeed begun planting a garden up on the hill beside the graves.

"He does such a good job at keeping himself busy," Ginny noted. "You were like that when you were a little boy too, Patrick."

Patrick looked out and took note of Caleb. Though he was keeping himself busy, he appeared to be looking for something or someone. Patrick knew who it was. The boy was looking for his friends who he would probably never see again. Patrick had helped release them from their trapped state of torment at the hands of the ghost of Pete Ables. Though Patrick was sad that Caleb had lost his friends, he was happy that the sweet little girls were no longer tormented and had crossed over to a much better place.

"It's the mountain air," said Blevins. "Studies have shown that fresh air and nature are wonderful for young children."

"That's interesting, Byron," Patrick said. "How did such factors affect you in your childhood?" Patrick smiled after the question. He knew Blevins would go on for at least an hour. Elizabeth seemed to be the only one who listened to him.

It was a good day and all was now well on Fork Mountain. Patrick found that with his sobriety the nightmares had stopped. He still dreamed of Samantha, but these were now pleasant dreams. He still tried to stay in bed as long as possible on weekends, hoping to extend the dreams.

When he was awake, he drew on his memories. He knew Samantha was in a better place. He didn't place any emphasis now on what might have happened to her. He knew she was happy. And he knew she was in good company.

He was in good company as well. He watched Caleb play in the field. He felt the cool, spring breeze blow on his face. He felt Heather's soft touch, taking his hand in hers, giving it a light squeeze. Life was good. He knew that with good health and good friends he would have all that he ever needed. He had learned to accept help from others in whatever form it came in. Even if that help came from the graves of babes.

The End

Printed in Great Britain
by Amazon